Finally, she slumped against him, her body spent.

She stayed there for a while, relishing the comfort of his strong arms around her, until she mustered the strength to regain control. "I'm sorry," she said.

"Don't you dare apologize. Anyone in your position would be upset. I'm a half step away from losing it myself."

His expression was a mixture of sympathy, worry and frustration, and Joelle's heart leaped at this man's honor and compassion.

He looked down at her and lifted one hand to wipe a tear from her cheek. "He will not hurt you or your sisters. I won't let that happen."

"I know," she said, and believed every word.

He stared at her a moment more and his expression shifted from frustration to something else.... Something she hadn't seen before. A shiver of excitement ran through her as she realized he was going to kiss her.

D0206168

THE REUNION

New York Times Bestselling Author
JANA DELEON

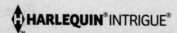

Recycling programs
for this product may
not exist in your area.

ISBN-13: 978-0-373-74773-3

THE REUNION

Copyright © 2013 by Jana DeLeon

Printed in U.S.A.

ABOUT THE AUTHOR

New York Times and *USA TODAY* bestselling author Jana DeLeon grew up among the bayous and small towns of southwest Louisiana. She's never actually found a dead body or seen a ghost, but she's still hoping. Jana started writing in 2001—she focuses on murderous plots set deep in the Louisiana bayous. By day she writes very boring technical manuals for a software company in Dallas. Visit Jana on her website, www.janadeleon.com.

Books by Jana DeLeon

HARLEQUIN INTRIGUE
1265—THE SECRET OF CYPRIERE BAYOU
1291—BAYOU BODYGUARD
1331—THE LOST GIRLS OF JOHNSON'S BAYOU
1380—THE RECKONING*
1386—THE VANISHING*
1393—THE AWAKENING*
1441—THE ACCUSED**
1447—THE BETRAYED**
1452—THE REUNION**

*Mystere Parish
**Mystere Parish: Family Inheritance

CAST OF CHARACTERS

Joelle LeBeau—The social worker specialized in helping women escape situations of domestic abuse, but her job was not without risk. One man will do anything to find his wife, whom Joelle helped hide. When she finds out that her stepfather died and the terms of her inheritance require her to spend two weeks at her childhood estate, it seems like perfect timing for her to disappear.

Tyler Duhon—He's back from the Middle East and attempting to gain his footing in the civilian world. His father, William, has other ideas. William wants Tyler to play bodyguard to the last of the LeBeau heirs. Tyler knows his father wouldn't ask if it wasn't important, so he can't say no. But he hopes the time passes quickly and the heiress doesn't bring as much trouble down on Calais as her sisters did.

Victor Brant—The abuser wants to find his wife in the worst way possible, and he's not going to let up on Joelle until he does exactly that. But did he follow her to Calais, or is someone else responsible for all the odd things happening at the LeBeau estate?

Mayor Dupree—The only time the old windbag isn't gossiping is when he's sleeping or eating, but does he know even more about Trenton Purcell and the situation with the inheritance than he's saying?

Bert Thibodeaux—Purcell promised the trucker he'd get a new rig when Purcell died, but the money wasn't Purcell's to give away and he knew it. The trucker is beyond angry, but is he angry enough to try to get revenge on the legitimate heirs?

Doctor Picard—The now-deceased physician had treated the heiress's mother over twenty years ago and had clearly been hiding something all these years. Was his secret worth killing over?

Chapter One

The woman stared out the second-story window of her mansion, looking across the overgrown driveway and down the lonely dirt road that led into town. Where had her children gone? Two were here before, then there were none. But the third... the third had never returned. Did she not know how much her mother loved her? Did she not know that only the thought of seeing her again kept the woman tied to this place?

A tear slid down the woman's cheek as the house began to fade away.

"I grow weak. Come to me, soon. Before it's too late."

JOELLE LEBEAU STOOD next to her ancient Honda Accord, certain it was totaled and not even wanting to think of replacing it. The two Jackson, Mississippi, policemen documented the vandalism, one with pen and paper and the other with a camera.

It was only 6:00 p.m., but the fall sunlight was

already fading, leaving the parking lot behind the Office of Social Services building dim. Joelle had been working late, as usual, when she heard a noise outside. By the time she'd removed her pistol from her desk drawer and peered out the back door into the parking lot, the vandal was already gone.

But he'd managed to do so much in so little time.

Every tire had been slashed and all the windows were shattered, leaving shards of glass littering the parking lot and the interior of the car. The windshield had a huge crack in the center that splintered out in every direction, and a message in dark red paint sprayed across it.

Destroyer.

That one word left her no doubt who had done the damage, and if she'd had trouble guessing, the note on the dashboard cinched it.

Give me what's mine.

One of the officers stepped up next to her. "You said you had someone in mind for this?"

She nodded. "Victor Brant."

The officer made a note. "Is he a client of yours?"

She almost laughed at the thought of the abusive, narcissistic Victor Brant admitting he needed help. "No. His wife is."

"And I take it Mr. Brant is unhappy with that?"

"He's unhappy with anyone who doesn't bow down to his every word or whose thoughts differ from his own. He's the worst type of abuser—

successful, good-looking and adored by his colleagues and in his community."

"So you're saying it would have been unlikely that people believed Mrs. Brant when she said her husband was abusive."

"She wasn't believed. The police were dispatched twice to their home. Both times, they declined to even take Mr. Brant in for questioning. In fact, the last time all they did was schedule a round of golf with Brant the following week at his country club."

The officer frowned. "The Jackson Police Department?"

"No. The Brants' estate is in Willow Grove. It was their local department. The mayor is Mr. Brant's first cousin. The chief of police is his uncle. Are you getting a clear picture?"

"Yes, ma'am, and I don't like it, but I can assure you that neither the mayor of Jackson nor the chief of police are interested in playing flunky to Mr. Brant. If he's responsible for this threat, he will be prosecuted. What I don't understand is this note."

He held up the note in a plastic baggie. "What do you have that he thinks belongs to him?"

Joelle took a deep breath and blew it out. "His wife."

The officer's eyes widened. "Excuse me?"

"In addition to my counseling job at the crisis center, I volunteer with an organization that helps women…quietly relocate, let's just say."

"An underground railroad?"

Joelle held in her frustration at the officer's obvious displeasure. Dedicated, honorable law enforcement professionals didn't like the vigilante-like tactics that the underground railroad organizations often used, but they had yet to offer a solution when their own departments couldn't keep women safe.

"There were no children," Joelle assured him. "And Ms. Brant left only with the clothes on her back and a watch that belonged to her mother. What we did was in no way illegal."

"Maybe not, but it's still not the usual way to get divorced."

"Look," she said, unable to control her aggravation any longer, "if any of us thought for a minute that Ms. Brant could simply file and get a divorce, like normal people do, she'd be staying at a Hilton, not hiding in a ten-by-ten room, afraid to even look out a window. Victor Brant said he'd kill her before he let her go. We have no reason to think he's lying."

The officer sighed and shook his head. "Assuming all of that is true, you haven't solved the problem. You've simply momentarily shifted Brant's focus from his wife to you. What makes you think you're any safer than she was?"

Despite the somewhat warm temperature of the fall evening, a chill passed over her and she crossed her arms across her chest. What he said was entirely correct, but it wasn't something she wanted to dwell on at the moment. When she'd decided on this profession and her volunteer work, Joelle invested time and money into her own safety. She lived in a well-lit condominium with a good security system. She spent at least an hour a week at the gun range and was a black belt.

"I'm safer, because I'm more qualified to handle this," she said finally. "It's my job to be prepared for these kinds of threats."

The officer didn't look convinced, but he closed the notebook and handed her a card. "If you receive any more threats, please contact me immediately. And be careful, Ms. LeBeau. Even the best trained among us can be gotten to. Can we give you a ride home?"

"No, thank you. A friend is coming to pick me up."

He nodded and climbed into his car with his partner. Joelle watched them exit the parking lot, then cast one more baleful glance at her junkyard-bound automobile. Sighing, she turned toward the office building, and when she did, she caught sight of movement out of the corner of her eye.

She spun around to peer at the Dumpster that rested in the corner of the parking lot against the fence. Nothing moved now, but she was certain something had just a second before.

You let that cop spook you.

Blowing out a breath, she hustled toward the back door of the office and let herself inside. Likely, it had just been an alley cat. Two or three regularly hung around the Dumpster, looking for an easy meal.

She pulled the dead bolt on the back door and hurried to the front of the office. Lisa would be here any moment to pick her up, and she didn't want her waiting too long. Her friend was an incredibly nice woman but a bit prone to dramatics and quite fearful of everything. Joelle had omitted the truth when she'd asked Lisa to give her lift, only citing car trouble as the reason for needing help.

As she walked through the office, she grabbed her purse from the desk where she'd dropped it earlier and continued through the reception area. As she approached the frosted glass door, a shadow moved in front of it and she drew up short.

The shadow stood for several seconds and Joelle dipped her hand into her purse and gripped her pistol. Then the shadow rapped on the door, causing her to jump.

"Anyone here? It's Myer's Courier Service. I have a package."

She hesitated just a second before releasing her pistol and stepping up to the door to unlock it. Myer's had delivered packages to the office many times before, but they usually made deliveries before the office closed for the day.

Peering out a tiny crack, she was relieved to see the same tall, skinny young man who always delivered. She pulled open the door and smiled at him.

"Hello, John. You almost missed me."

John handed her a legal-sized envelope and produced a clipboard for her to sign. "I know I'm late," he said, flushing a bit. "I had a flat tire and it took longer to change it out than I thought it would."

"Well, I'm glad you're fixed now. How's Janey doing her first semester of college?" John's sister had volunteered at the crisis center her senior year of high school.

"She'd doing fine. She's working with disabled kids two days a week after class."

Joelle smiled. "That's great. Tell her we miss her and good luck."

"Yes, ma'am," he said and left.

She closed the door and placed the package on the secretary's desk, but as she started to walk away, the name on the package caught her eye. Joelle LeBeau.

Frowning, she picked up the package again. It was unusual for her to receive a courier delivery. The secretary usually dealt with all incoming paperwork and orders. She glanced at the return address and sucked in a breath.

Calais, Louisiana.

She studied the return address more closely. What in the world would an attorney in Calais want with her? She was only four years old when her mother died and she was sent to live with distant cousins in Mississippi, but certain moments of her childhood on the LeBeau estate were etched in her mind, with recall so vivid it was as if she were watching it take place on a television. For years, she'd tried to convince herself to visit Calais—to confront her stepfather, the man who cast off the three sisters—but every time she approached the entry for the highway to New Orleans, she drove past it.

Not ready to face those vivid memories yet.

She tore open the envelope and pulled out a letter, already certain she didn't want to hear anything her stepfather had to say. If Trenton Purcell was on his deathbed and begging forgiveness, she'd raise a glass and toast, but she'd never accept an apology for what he did.

As she began to read, her pulse ticked up until she could feel it beating in her temples. Her evil stepfather was dead. He had been much older than her mother, so Joelle knew the day would come sooner than later, but she'd never expected to be notified of the event.

Then she read the second paragraph and sank down onto the desktop, her knees weak. It was all theirs. The estate, the fortune—everything her mother and her mother's ancestors had built—it all belonged to Ophelia LeBeau's three daughters.

Purcell hadn't been able to control the fortune after his death.

She continued reading and frowned. In order to inherit, she had to spend two straight weeks on the estate, to be verified by the local sheriff. Her two sisters, Alaina and Danae, had already completed their two weeks and were anxious to meet her.

A wave of excitement rushed over her, then a flash of anxiety. All these years, she'd wanted to meet her sisters, but hadn't even known where to start looking. Now they were waiting for her at their childhood home—waiting for her to come fulfill a rather bizarre inheritance request so that they could finally claim their birthright.

But that meant not only returning to Calais, but staying in that house. The house with bad memories.

A mental image of her vandalized car flashed through her mind. Maybe leaving Jackson for a couple of weeks wasn't a bad idea. It might give Brant a chance to realize that the Jackson Police Department wasn't for sale like the one in Willow Grove. She had plenty of vacation coming. In fact, she hadn't taken more than a day off at a time since she'd started working at the crisis center over five years ago.

A horn honked outside and she stuffed the letter into her purse and swung the strap over her shoulder before hurrying out of the office. She'd call

William Duhon, the attorney who'd sent the letter, first thing in the morning. Then she'd call her boss to say she was taking a long overdue vacation…for the long overdue purpose of addressing her past.

Chapter Two

Tyler Duhon stared in dismay across the café table at his father, William, Calais's resident attorney. Not even Johnny's absolutely stellar banana pudding could sweeten Tyler's disposition toward what his father had just asked him to do.

"No way," Tyler said. "Look, I promise I'm not going to be lying around on your couch all day for months on end. I'll be starting my own security firm as soon as I get all the permits and approved formation documents."

William pushed his empty bowl to the edge of the table and took another sip of coffee. "I'm not worried about my couch. Your mother picked it out and I never liked it much—all those roses. And I'm well aware of your business pursuits as I filed the corporate formation documents for you last week."

"Then what's your angle?"

"I don't have an angle. What I have is a spooky, partially repaired old house that has three deaths attached to it in as many months, and an heir who needs to occupy that house for two weeks in order to gain back everything that was stolen from her. I'd really like her to have an easier go of it than her sisters did."

Tyler frowned. The happenings surrounding Trenton Purcell's death and the subsequent arrival of two of Ophelia LeBeau's daughters had set off a chain reaction of threats, break-ins, stalkers and eventually, three deaths—one murder and two in self-defense. But the facts paled in comparison to the sheer amount of disturbance that had rocked the sleepy bayou town.

"I'm not sure what you think I can do," Tyler said finally.

"You plan on opening a security firm, don't you? I expect you can protect the heiress and her assets. I'm not expecting you to do so for free. The estate will be happy to cover the cost of on-site security—in fact, in light of recent events, they're requiring it."

Tyler shook his head. "I'm opening a firm, but I'm not going to do any of the face-to-face work. I'm focusing solely on hardware and administration. I'll hire some of my military buddies for the groundwork."

William scrunched his brow. "You plan on sitting behind a desk all day? You'll be bored within a week."

I don't think so.

"If I get bored," Tyler said, "we'll go shopping for a new couch. Mom's been gone for years. It's time you got some manly furniture in the place."

William studied him, and Tyler forced himself not to squirm under his father's scrutiny. Apparently, his attempt at levity hadn't distracted his father for a moment. Tyler had never been able to hide anything from the shrewd attorney, who seemed to possess the ability to read minds. And more than anyone, his father knew how much Tyler hated sitting still—hated concentrating on paper and numbers and words. He was smart, but it had been a struggle to get him out of high school. He'd sit in class almost twitching with anxiety, wanting desperately to jump out a window and run until he sated his body's always-demanding call to action.

It's why he'd joined the Marine Corps as soon as he graduated.

The Marine Corps had immediately recognized that Tyler was able to sit still long enough to take a flight to where they needed him for action. Beyond that, and you risked a fidgety bored adult, carrying a weapon and expertly trained at using it. When Tyler wasn't on maneuvers in the Middle East, he worked in the villages alongside the occupants, helping them rebuild their homes. He hadn't sat behind a desk since high school, and he already knew he was going to be bored.

But you rarely saw people die when you sat behind a desk.

And that was the bottom line. He'd seen too much sadness, too much tragedy, and he needed to get away from it all. Which was why he was digging in his heels over the issue with the heiress. The last thing he wanted to do was sit all day in that monstrosity of a house with some fainting violet of a woman.

"I don't know what happened overseas," William said quietly, cutting into his thoughts. "I'd like to think that someday you'll tell me. But I wouldn't ask this of you if I had other options. The reality is, you're the best person for the job and I need the best. This woman's safety is on my conscience. I can't rest if she's not protected."

Tyler held in a sigh, knowing he'd just lost the fight, but determined to give it one last parting shot. "What about Carter? He's definitely capable, and his mother would make him do anything for you."

William nodded. "Quite true, which is why Carter was tasked with verifying the daily presence of all the heirs. But Carter is Calais's sheriff, and lately, that job is more than full-time. Not to mention that he has a new fiancée who lives with him, and it would be highly inappropriate for him to move in with her sister—even if only for two weeks and for the purpose of protecting her."

Tyler's parting shot faded into the distance, and

he let out the sigh. If anyone but William had tried such a line on him, he would have accused them of attempting to guilt him into doing what they wanted, but that was something his father would never do. Which was why Tyler knew William was telling the truth when he said the woman's safety weighed on his conscience. His father was a good man—the best, actually—and he wasn't afraid to care about people.

Even if it cost him in the long run.

"Fine," Tyler relented. "I'll do it. But only for the two weeks the estate requires her to be there. If she wants to stay and redecorate or open a knitter's colony or something, she's on her own. And I have no intention of sitting and staring at her all day. You want me in the house, that's fine, but I want to talk to the contractor and get a list of things I can work on while I'm there."

William beamed at him. "Thank you, Tyler. I'm sure Zach can provide you with plenty of items that need attention."

Tyler nodded. Zach Sargent was the contractor William had hired to make repairs on the house, but he'd had other reasons for coming to Calais. Zach's father, a funeral director, was one of the many people Purcell had paid off, and Zach took the job in order to figure out exactly what his father's attempted deathbed confession and the large cash deposit had entailed. Zach hadn't gotten the answers he'd hoped for, but he'd formed a relationship with the youngest of Ophelia's daughters and had moved back to New Orleans, with her in tow. He returned to Calais on weekends to continue repairs on the house.

"You don't know how relieved I am that you'll be my eyes and ears in that house," William said.

"Why? Surely, it's all over now."

William's smile faded away and he shook his head. "Much of Purcell's evil intentions and those who carried them out have been exposed, that's true."

"But?"

"But I still have a bad feeling about all of it."

"Of course you do. Purcell was a hit man for the New Orleans mafia who romanced Ophelia Le-Beau for her money and a safe hiding place when his own employer put a hit on him. Then he killed her and sent her kids away like they were department store returns. I've got lots of feelings about it myself, and trust me, all of them are bad."

"We don't know for certain that Purcell killed Ophelia."

"Then what was he paying all those people for?"

William nodded. "Oh, we're certain Purcell was paying for silence, and I'd guess it's exactly as you say and he killed Ophelia, but we still can't prove it. And with everyone on his payroll dead, there's no one left to ask."

"And that's exactly my original point—all the bad guys are dead."

William stared out the plate-glass window of the café and looked across the street into the swamp. Finally, he looked back at Tyler and leaned across the table.

"I don't think they are *all* dead." William's voice was barely more than a whisper. "The swamp is wrong. You don't even have to enter it to feel it. Something is still out of balance, and I don't think the swamp will rest until it churns up all its secrets."

If it were anyone else speaking or if his father were talking about anywhere else but Calais, Tyler would suggest he needed professional help. But the swamps of Mystere Parish were different than any place he'd ever been. Although he'd been surrounded by them his entire childhood, and had traipsed through them thousands of hours, Tyler had never felt at ease in the dense cypress trees and foliage.

It was as if the swamp itself was alive.

Certainly, the swamp comprised lots of living things, but it was something more than that—as if the swamp were a separate living entity, with its own agenda. At times, it was pleasant enough, but he'd never found the atmosphere relaxing, even though parts of it were beautiful. At other times, it had been oppressive, the weight of it pressing in around him.

That oppressive weight had always aligned with something tragic, usually death.

If the swamp was out of balance, then something was still very wrong in Calais. Given that the only recent tragedies all centered on the LeBeau estate, Tyler understood why his father was so anxious to ensure that Ophelia's middle daughter was offered the best protection he could provide. The swamp wouldn't return to a peaceful state until a reckoning had occurred.

"What do you think is wrong?" Tyler asked.

"I don't know, and that's what bothers me the most. But we may get some answers soon."

"How's that?"

His father looked at him, his expression sad and haunting. "We're exhuming Ophelia LeBeau tomorrow."

Chapter Three

As she pulled through Calais, Joelle studied the old buildings, looking for something that appeared familiar. The weathered brick buildings were typical of any old small town, but none of them sparked even a twitch of memory. The café caught her interest as she pulled by, but only because she planned to spend her two weeks allowing others to cook for her. She hoped the food was good, as it appeared to be the only option.

Her stomach rumbled as her thoughts turned to food, and she realized it was well past lunch. She'd almost stopped several times, but each time she pressed the accelerator and continued down the highway, anxious to get the long drive over with. Unfortunately, she had arranged to meet the attorney at the house in about ten minutes, so eating would have to wait a bit longer.

As soon as she passed the last building on Main Street, she pulled a paper with directions from her purse. She'd gotten this far without referring to the attorney's instructions, but when the directions started including items such as "turn right at the giant oak tree," it was time to pay attention. The last thing she wanted to do was to get lost in the swamp.

She turned to the right at a four-way stop, directing her car onto a semblance of a road. The economy rental she'd acquired before leaving Jackson was no match for the bumps and holes that mostly made up the dirt trail that led to the house, and she gritted her teeth as the dashboard rattled. She swerved to miss a huge hole, but her right front tire caught the edge of it and the entire car dropped. Cringing at the sound of the bottom of the car sliding across rocks, she clenched the steering wheel and leaned forward to get a better look at the road.

The cypress trees that lined both sides of the road grew thicker, creating a canopy above the road that blocked most of the sunlight from entering. If she hadn't known any better, she would have sworn it was late evening rather than mid-afternoon. Surely, the house couldn't be much farther.

Fifteen minutes later, she rounded a corner and the house burst into view. Continuing her slow creep around what remained of the circular driveway, she looked up at the place she'd spent the first four years of her life, waiting for that spark of recognition to hit. She was disappointed when it never came.

A new pickup truck was parked in front of the house, and she pulled up behind it and parked, figuring it belonged to the attorney. She jumped out of the car and stretched her aching legs and cast a glance back at the car. She'd rented the economy vehicle to try it out, thinking she might purchase the same model to replace her totaled Honda. The tiny car would be a huge benefit in the city, where she rarely drove more than twenty miles in one stretch, but after hours on the road, she was well aware of just how cramped her long legs were in such a compact space.

Her suitcases could wait until after she'd spoken to the attorney, so she headed up to the front door. When she raised her hand and knocked, the door inched forward just a bit. She pushed the door open and stuck her head inside.

"Mr. Duhon," she called out. "It's Joelle Le-Beau."

She waited a bit, expecting the attorney to appear or at least respond, but only her own voice echoed through the giant entry. Deciding the attorney must be off in a part of the house where he couldn't hear her, she stepped inside, then drew up short. A twinge of something—some tiny flicker of recognition—flashed through her, but as soon as she tried to grasp it, the flicker disappeared.

The entry was massive, like the entry of a hotel or museum. The giant spiral staircase was centered toward the front and she peered up to see the balcony running around the entire second floor, doors to various rooms lining the upstairs walls. The first floor of the entry was littered—there wasn't really a better word—with decorative columns and tables, all housing art, china and glass that seemed to have no consistency of era or country of origin.

To the left, a wide hallway led away from the entry. Patches of sunlight streamed from the room at the end of the hallway and onto the stone floor. Figuring the hallway led to a family room or kitchen, she took off to the left, hoping to locate the attorney.

The kitchen and breakfast nook were in sharp contrast to the rest of the house and had her smiling. Clearly, someone had put in long hours on this room and it showed—the gleaming cabinets, polished countertops and fresh coat of paint made the room a cheery retreat from the gloomy entry. Giant windows formed the far wall, along with a single door that led onto an overgrown patio.

She gazed around the room once more before readying herself to continue her search for the attorney, and that's when she realized the patio door was partially open. Now understanding why the attorney hadn't heard her call out in the entry, she stepped outside and looked up and down the long stone patio. Shrubs and brush had grown right up to the edges, and vines climbed the stone columns and trailed across the ground, but it was clear that someone had recently started clearing the brush away.

Following a trail of small branches and leaves, she walked to the far end of the patio and saw the tiny path that led straight into the swamp. The remnants of foliage continued down the path, but Joelle hesitated before stepping off the stone patio. Something about the swamp bothered her—more than just the dim, creepy appearance.

She was just about to head back inside and wait for the attorney when a voice sounded behind her and she jumped, her foot slipping off the edge of the patio and onto the path several inches below. She struggled to maintain her balance, but the drop was just enough to send her crashing into the brush at the side of the trail.

As soon as she hit the ground, she scrambled to get up, fighting the thick vines that she'd brought down on top of her. Suddenly, she felt someone grasp her arm and tug her completely to her feet. A branch slapped her across the face and her eyes watered, so the only thing she could make out when she was upright was a tall man with dark hair.

Brad.

Instantly, a mental image of her ex-boyfriend flashed across her mind, and just as quickly, she sent it scurrying to the recesses where it belonged. Brad was long gone and old news.

She blinked a couple of times and the man came into focus, but this young, incredibly gorgeous and seriously ripped man couldn't possibly be the aging attorney she'd talked to on the phone. The scowl on his face was just further proof. The attorney had been kind and cheerful. This man looked like those attributes were not part of his makeup.

"I hope you're not always this jumpy," he said. "A fall in the horror funhouse could bring more than just vines crashing down around you."

A blush ran up her neck and onto her face, and she felt a flash of heat wash over her. "Maybe if you didn't go sneaking up behind people, you wouldn't startle them."

He raised his eyebrows, looking almost amused at her accusation. "I'm wearing work boots, and I was hardly tiptoeing across that patio. Hell, people back in town could hear me coming."

"Really? Then maybe you should tell them why you're trespassing on private property."

He sighed. "You must be Joelle. My father owes me big-time for this."

Joelle narrowed her eyes at him. "Exactly who is your father?"

"William Duhon."

"Oh," she said, momentarily taken aback that the pleasant gentleman she'd spoken to on the phone had produced such a surly son. "Your father was supposed to meet me here. Is he on his way?"

"He's not coming."

"What do you mean? He's supposed to provide me a key to the house and go over any of my questions concerning the estate requirements."

"Well, you got me instead." He pulled a giant iron key from his pocket and handed it to her. "That's the front door key. I'm having keys to the patio and back door duplicated and will pick them up this afternoon."

"Am I supposed to meet your father at his office?"

If possible, he looked even more aggrieved.

"No. I'm supposed to take you to meet him for an early supper at the café, after I get you settled in."

She stared. Was he joking? The last thing she intended to do was get in a car with Mr. Personality.

"I'm sure I can find my way back to the café, the same way I found the house," she said. "I don't need an escort."

"My father says you do, and unfortunately for me and you, so does the estate. During your two-week stay in Calais, I will go wherever you go."

"That's outrageous! Neither the estate nor your father can mandate who I spend my time with."

"No, but they can insist you maintain personal security at all times, and they have."

"What in the world for? To protect me from the clutter and dust I saw in there? The only risk to my

safety so far has been you, and I'm supposed to believe you were assigned to protect me?"

He clenched his jaw and she could tell she'd in-
sulted him, just as she'd intended.

"Well," he said, "I managed to sneak up on you
in broad daylight wearing construction boots, right?
I'm guessing that makes my observation skills a
sight better than your own."

He whirled around and strode away from her.

"I'll get your things out of your car," he mum-
bled as he left.

Joelle stared behind him wondering if the entire
world had gone crazy.

I will go wherever you go.

She stiffened. Surely that didn't mean he was
staying in the house with her. Granted, she had her
apprehensions about staying in the spooky, rambling mansion alone, but if the choice were Mr.
Personality or the ghosts, she'd definitely take the
ghosts.

TYLER STALKED AROUND the side of the house to the
front where Joelle's car was parked. She'd left it
unlocked, which surprised him at first given that
his father said she was some sort of social worker,
but then she probably figured no one was roaming this far out in the swamp looking to lift items
from a car.

If only she were right. Then he'd be sitting on

his dad's couch watching television instead of fending off insults.

Likely, no one would lift items from her car, but if his father's instincts were correct, someone was still roaming around the estate. At least this time, a full-time security detail was on-site and prepared for battle. Tyler wasn't about to let someone get the better of him in his own neck of the woods.

He grabbed two suitcases from the backseat of the car and carried them inside, still trying to figure out how he was supposed to manage two full weeks around Joelle LeBeau. When his father told him Joelle was a social worker, Tyler had formed a mental picture of some motherly-type woman—probably heavyset—and with a kind smile.

The tall, curvy Creole beauty he'd pulled out of the bushes was the last thing he'd ever expected and, certainly, the last thing he wanted. Gorgeous, endangered women were part of a past he intended to put far behind him, which was precisely the reason he wanted to sit at a desk until he passed out from boredom. During his eight years in the Middle East, he'd had enough excitement to last a lifetime.

During the last twelve months, he'd had enough beautiful women to last ten lifetimes.

Chapter Four

Joelle looked across the table at William Duhon, as charmed by the aging attorney as she was frustrated by his son. Clearly, Tyler hadn't inherited any of his father's charisma. Her private security detail hadn't spoken a word during the entire drive into Calais, and after arriving at the café, had opened his mouth only long enough to tell his father that he needed to pick up some supplies at the general store and would meet them back at the café in an hour or so. William appeared a bit embarrassed by his son's behavior, but just nodded and directed her to a booth in the far corner.

"I apologize for the rather unconventional meeting location," William said, "but I recall you saying when you called from New Orleans that you hadn't stopped to eat. I figured we could accomplish two things at once."

Joelle took another bite of sirloin steak, smothered in gravy and onions, and said a silent prayer of thanks that she hadn't stopped for fast food on the way to Calais.

"It was worth the wait," she said.

William smiled. "Johnny's mother was the best cook in Calais. When he opened this place, it was with the intention to use only her recipes, and he's kept it that way for thirty years."

"If it's not broken…"

"Quite so. Johnny's made a good business here. Most everyone has at least a couple meals a week at the café. Make sure you save some room for banana pudding. That's the dessert special today."

"Banana pudding?" She looked down at her plate. "Maybe I'll take half of this home for supper. I may have to start jogging while I'm here."

William pointed out the plate-glass window to a building across the street. "I'm convinced that this café is the reason the seamstress shop stays in business—letting out waistbands and such."

"It probably won't come to that. My brief glance at the downstairs of the house provided a mental list of things to do that is as long as the Mississippi. I won't have any problem getting my exercise in."

Quite frankly, the state of the house had surprised her more than anything else she'd heard so far. She never expected that her stepfather would keep it up, but he'd been dead for months. Surely, the estate could afford to hire a cleaning service.

"Can I ask a question?" she asked.

"Of course. That's what I'm here for."

"Can the estate hire someone to help with the cleaning? Even if I worked on it full-time for two weeks, I couldn't put a dent in it."

William sighed. "The big services in New Orleans won't travel this far out for the job, especially with no hotel to place the crew in. I've hired several local women, but they never last more than a day."

"Why not? Surely, jobs are hard to come by here."

"Absolutely, and they could all use the money, but they were too afraid to continue working."

"Afraid of what?"

"They claim they saw a ghost."

Joelle stared. "You're serious?"

"Yes." William frowned and hesitated a moment before continuing. "There's been some unpleasantness surrounding the house."

"What do you mean?"

"Your sister Alaina had a stalker who tried to kill her. Sheriff Carter Trahan, now Alaina's fiancé, shot and killed him in the front drive of the house."

"Oh, my! Alaina is all right, though?"

"She's fine. After all that was put to rest, we hoped Danae would have an easier time with her two weeks, but a different set of problems surfaced."

William took a deep breath and blew it out before continuing. "I don't know how to say this in a good way, so I'm just going to lay out the facts. Your stepfather used estate money to buy assets and then sell them. He had the authority to use estate money to purchase investment property—such as art—but could not request cash withdrawals outside of a small living allowance."

"So that's why we still have an estate to inherit," Joelle said, one of her questions answered. "I wondered about that."

William nodded. "Danae accepted contract work with the estate to go through all the paperwork in the house, and she located some of Purcell's personal accounting records. The records show large cash receipts, which we think are from the sale of the assets acquired using estate money, but they also show large cash disbursements."

"I thought he became a hermit after we left. What was he purchasing?"

"Part of the money spent was on you girls."

"Us? I doubt that. Purcell hated us. Even as young as I was, I could feel it."

"No doubt you're right." William paused for a couple of seconds and frowned. "Your adoptive parents passed away, correct?"

Joelle nodded. "They were already in their fifties when they took me in. They'd never been able to have their own children, and even though they knew it would be a struggle at their age, keeping up with such a young child, they knew it was their last chance at being parents."

William's expression softened. "They were good people, then?"

"The best. Of course, I would rather have been with my mother and sisters, but given the circumstances, I couldn't have asked for a better place to go."

"I, uh, don't want to do anything to diminish your opinion in any way, but it appears that Purcell paid each family twenty thousand dollars to take you girls in."

Suddenly, something Joelle had never understood clicked. "My college fund."

"What do you mean?"

"My adoptive parents didn't make a lot of money. I always assumed I'd need loans to pay for college, but they established a fund for me when I came to live with them. I've seen the records. They opened the account with twenty thousand dollars. I always wondered where it came from."

William's relief was apparent. "That's wonderful. Just wonderful."

"You said part of the money was spent on the families that took us in. What else did he pay for?"

"I apologize in advance, because this is most distressing, but we suspect he paid for silence. So far, we've discovered payments to the man who pronounced your mother's death and the funeral director in New Orleans who handled her burial."

A wave of nausea rolled over Joelle as William's words clicked in her mind. "No, you're not saying..."

"I'm so sorry to have to tell you this," William said, "but we think Purcell killed your mother to get control of her money. He probably didn't know that the terms of the estate would prevent him from taking control of the cash."

Her chest felt as if an entire city block had been dropped on it. She tried to concentrate on controlling her breathing, but every intake of air felt as if a burning dagger stabbed her lungs. Her mind slipped to the past and she steeled herself for the vision that would surely come.

"Are you all right?"

William's voice seemed far away, and it took her several seconds to force herself back to the present—back to Johnny's Café in Calais. She couldn't afford to slip into the past, especially not to the dark place. Not if she had any intention of making it the two weeks she needed to fulfill the estate requirements.

She took a big drink of water and nodded. "I'm okay. It's just shocking."

"It is," William agreed. "I still have my moments when I think it all must be a mistake, but the facts all seem to point that way, especially as one of the men Purcell paid kidnapped Danae and tried to kill her."

Joelle's heart dropped once more at the thought of her baby sister kidnapped and fighting for her life. "I can't believe it. It's like something out of a movie."

"Perhaps, if it's a horror movie. Of course, there's quite a bit more research to be done as we try to get to the bottom of things. Danae is still going through household records...there's something else."

Joelle stiffened, not certain she wanted to hear anything else. If William's hesitation was any indication, then what he was about to tell her wasn't going to be any better than what she was already trying to absorb.

"How much more can there be?"

"This is a big one, I'm afraid. Given that there's mostly only circumstantial evidence and hearsay as to Purcell's crimes, your sisters requested that your mother be exhumed."

Joelle stared. "They're hoping to find evidence of murder. After all these years, is that even possible?"

"Anything's possible, although it's probably not likely. But Alaina and Danae felt they had to try everything. They would have waited for you to make the decision but, at the time, I had no idea how long it would take to locate you."

Joelle waved a hand in dismissal. "I don't mind

any of that. I agree with their choice. I want answers as much as they do."

"That's a relief. I'm sorry to dump all this on you the second you arrive. Your sisters planned to tell you everything when you met, but I asked them to allow me to speak to you instead. I didn't want your reunion marred by all this unpleasantness. I want you girls to focus on getting to know one another again."

Joelle smiled at William, his thoughtfulness such a departure from the people she normally dealt with. "Has anyone told you how wonderful you are, William?"

The attorney blushed a bit. "Just doing my job."

"We both know you're doing far more than that. I remember you said someone would verify my presence on the estate each day. Will you be doing that or will Tyler report to you?"

"Actually, Carter Trahan has an agreement with the estate to perform the verification duties for all three of you. Given everything that's happened, he's also busy trying to investigate Purcell and those who may have been on his payroll."

"Carter is the sheriff, right?"

William nodded. "And will become your brother-in-law next year."

Joelle struggled to wrap her mind around it all. Two sisters, a future brother-in-law, a potential fortune and a sulking bodyguard. Only the bodyguard ruined the perfect picture.

That, and kidnapping, and attempted murder.

Before she could change her mind, Joelle launched into her next set of questions. "Your son... Tyler...I get the impression he's not overly happy with his job."

William sighed. "I noticed his manners weren't exactly up to par when you arrived. I apologize that he didn't provide a warm welcome."

"He's a grown man. You don't need to apologize for him."

"In this case I do, as I'm responsible for putting him in a position he didn't want to be in. Given everything that has happened with your sisters, the estate insisted on twenty-four-hour, on-site security for you, and I put pressure on Tyler to provide it."

"After everything you've told me, I completely understand the estate's position, but why Tyler? If he doesn't want to do it, why did you pressure him to?"

"Because he's the best man for the job," William said simply. "Tyler was a securities expert for the Marine Corps. He kept entire military bases safe while ferreting out the secrets of the enemy. If he can't protect you, I'm not sure anyone can."

Some of Tyler's stiff, direct approach to things now made sense. "He was in the Middle East?"

William nodded.

"How long?"

"Eight years. He arrived back in the States only two weeks ago. He's starting a private security firm as soon as the formation documents are approved by the state."

"Well," Joelle said, processing all this new information. "I suppose tolerating a bit of a grouch is a small cost for the level of protection I'm getting in return."

William gave her a small smile. "He wasn't always this grouchy. His time overseas changed him, but he won't talk about it."

The attorney sighed. "I'm sure he saw horrific things. Hearing about them on the news is bad enough, but to see it firsthand and then feel some level of responsibility because it happened… I imagine it's a lot of weight for any man."

Instantly, Joelle's training kicked in and she slipped directly into psychologist mode, momentarily chiding herself for making something personal when that was rarely the case. "I'm sure you're right. So what can I do to make the transition easier?"

"Communicate your plans with him and don't try to fight his presence, even though I'm sure it will feel awkward and inconvenient at times. Allow him to do physical labor. He's not made for sitting behind a desk, although he thinks that's what he needs to do. Movement keeps his mind focused and his body ready for action. He's been that way his entire life."

Joelle nodded. "He was clearing brush from the back patio when I arrived. Now that I think about it, I suppose it was a two-point process—he worked off some energy, and the more brush that's cleared away from the house, the easier it will be to see someone approaching."

William's expression softened and his eyes misted up just a bit. "Your mother would be so happy to see how you girls turned out. Despite all the obstacles placed in your path, you're all self-confident, intelligent and compassionate. She couldn't have asked for more."

A blush ran up her neck at William's compliments. "Thank you. It's so nice to finally talk to people who knew my mother, and I can't wait to meet Alaina and Danae."

"They're visiting this afternoon?"

"Yes. Alaina was in New Orleans on business, but she is going to pick up Danae and they'll both be here late this evening. They have to be back in New Orleans tomorrow, so we're planning a slumber party."

"How delightful!"

Joelle nodded, hoping the attorney was right. More than anything in the world, she wanted to meet her sisters, but the reality was, she was nervous. Based on everything she'd heard, Danae and

Alaina had already formed a close bond. What if they didn't like her? What if the passage of time had removed that connection between them?

She took a big sip of water and told herself to relax. Her sisters were alive and well and spending a night with her catching up. In two weeks, all of them would inherit everything that was temporarily stolen from them.

Nothing or no one was going to put a damper on her happiness.

TYLER PICKED UP a bag of chocolate chip cookies and a six-pack of beer and set them on the counter in the general store. The owner, Samuel, was tied up in the back helping a man load his new lawn mower onto his truck, so Tyler leaned back against the counter and grabbed a hunting magazine to flip through while he waited.

"Only two weeks out of the Corps and you already have bachelor shopping down," a voice sounded in front of him.

Tyler looked up at a grinning Carter Trahan.

Despite Tyler's general disgust at his current predicament, he couldn't help but smile as he shook Carter's extended hand.

"I'm sorry I missed you when you came by my dad's house," Tyler said.

Carter waved his hand in dismissal. "You're working on your business stuff. I'm working on solving ancient murders. I knew we'd run into each other eventually."

"I guess it's hard to go too long without seeing someone in a town as small as Calais."

Carter nodded. "It's certainly a different pace than New Orleans. I imagine you're in an even bigger culture shock, relocating from a war zone halfway across the world."

"It's been…interesting. Sometimes I still have these moments of panic, where I think there's something I was supposed to do that I didn't."

"I know exactly what you mean. Between the caseload and the constantly increasing paperwork requirements, New Orleans cops are to the point of needing personal secretaries to keep up."

"Do you ever miss it?"

"I did a little at first. It was too slow, too quiet and I think I spent a lot of time feeling guilty because it was too easy."

"Trenton Purcell's death seems to have changed all that."

"You got that right. If anyone had told me before I came here that this much crime—running this far back—could happen in a place like Calais, I would have laughed. It's hard to believe one man can cause such a ripple of crime that lasted past his own death."

Tyler nodded, thinking about everything his father had told him about the situation. "My dad told me you found out Purcell was a hit man and probably took up with Ophelia for a place to hide."

"Yeah, at first I thought Purcell married her figuring he could get Ophelia to move away from Louisiana, but with everything I know now, I'm guessing he planned to kill her from the beginning. He wouldn't have known about the will. He probably assumed he'd get everything when she was gone. When I think about everything those girls lost because of him…"

Tyler felt a flicker of guilt over the terse way he'd handled meeting Joelle. She and her sisters were the living victims in the middle of this mess. She certainly hadn't asked for her mother to be murdered and for her stepfather to send her off to strangers. He'd been so busy worrying about his own needs that he hadn't really stopped to consider how difficult this must be for her—for all of them.

"Alaina and Danae are fine, right?" Tyler asked. "I mean…considering everything that's happened."

"They are both incredibly strong women," Carter said, and Tyler could hear the admiration in his voice. "Most people would have crumbled under the stress of the discoveries alone, much less the attempts on their lives. But those two just got mad and more determined."

Tyler smiled. "You have to admire that."

"Definitely. It helps that they have each other.

They're thick as thieves. You'd never know they spent most of their lives apart."

"Hopefully Joelle will fit as well with them."

"I don't think they're going to give her a choice. Your dad tells me he's got you on security detail."

Tyler sighed. "I tried to get out of it, but you know Dad."

Carter laughed. "Oh, yeah, I know your dad. Between him and my mom, I could be talked into most anything. This whole mess started for me when your dad asked me to play hall monitor. I ended up with a kidnapping, three deaths and a fiancée."

Tyler winced at the fiancée part of Carter's statement. "I'm not looking to acquire any of those on my Calais service record, especially the last one."

Carter grinned. "And you think I was? Have you met Joelle yet?"

"Yeah, she arrived this afternoon. I brought her to town for a meeting with my dad at the café."

"So how does she look?"

Tyler shrugged, not about to go into details of the delicious Joelle with Carter. "She looks like a woman."

Carter's grin widened. "That good, huh?"

"I didn't say anything like that."

"You didn't have to. I know both her sisters, and I know that look. I used to wear it. Joelle is a knock-out and that pisses you off even more."

Tyler sighed. "Remind me again why we're friends?"

Carter laughed and clapped Tyler's back. "Because I keep you honest."

"Is that even possible?" A man's voice boomed from behind them.

Tyler turned around as Mayor James Dupree stepped up to him, his hand extended.

"It's good to have you home," Mayor Dupree said. "I know your daddy must be relieved."

"Yes, sir, I imagine he is." Tyler shook the man's hand and hoped that he had an appointment that didn't allow him to hang around for long. Mayor Dupree was a marathon talker and had never once said anything even remotely interesting.

"Good to see you, Carter." Mayor Dupree nodded. "How's that pretty fiancée of yours doing?"

"She's fine, sir," Carter replied and rolled his eyes at Tyler as soon as Mayor Dupree looked away.

"Good, good," Mayor Dupree said and studied Tyler again. "So what will you be doing now that you're home?"

"I'm opening a security firm. Maybe city hall can use my services."

The mayor laughed. "Well, we're still holding council meetings at the café, so you'd have to wait until we build a city hall. I hope you have some other clients in mind, as that might be a while in coming."

"Actually, I'm doing some work for my dad."

"The LeBeau estate?"

"Yes."

The mayor shook his head. "That has been such an unfortunate set of circumstances. I never would have imagined such things could happen in Calais."

Carter cleared his throat. "I thought you and Roger Martin were friends from way back. I would have figured you'd know if he was plotting things with Trenton Purcell."

Mayor Dupree sighed. "I wish I had known. Maybe I could have talked him out of it. Maybe all this would have turned out differently."

"Maybe," Carter said. "You know, I'm pretty sure Purcell had more than just Roger on his payroll. Since you were around then, maybe you'd have an idea who I should take a closer look at."

"I wish I did, and I'll be sure to let you know if I think of something. Well, I've got to run. You two stay out of trouble." He gave them a nod and hustled out of the store quicker than Tyler thought his flabby frame would allow.

Tyler stared after him and frowned. "Should I be happy he didn't stick around and talk us to death, or suspicious and wonder why?"

"Number two."

"Any particular reason other than him being friends with Roger?"

"Yeah. If Joelle doesn't make her two weeks,

the city of Calais inherits millions' worth of Le-Beau assets."

"You think he knows that?"

"Do you?"

"The way he left… Wow, all that money and under the control of the good mayor," Tyler said, a whole new train of thought opened up with that bit of information. "My dad really needs to learn to talk more about things that matter."

Carter smiled. "Come on, I'll buy you a root beer float and we can talk about your ideas for security now that you've seen the house, and I can try to fill in any blanks that William might have left."

Tyler checked his watch but figured his dad and Joelle would probably be a while longer. Besides, the general store had an old-fashioned soda fountain with the best root beer floats in the South, and he did have some things he wanted to run by Carter after seeing the house. His friend had suggested a casual planning meeting over a drink, but Tyler could tell Carter was worried, and Carter Trahan was the last person to go off on a tangent.

Maybe his dad was right. Maybe it wasn't over.

Chapter Five

Joelle pushed her feet against the floorboard of Tyler's truck, wishing he could navigate the bumpy road at a faster pace. She'd been finishing up with William when her cell phone rang with Alaina's call. Her sisters had forgotten to call when they left New Orleans and had lost cell service not far outside of the city. By the time she'd gotten a signal again, Alaina was only ten minutes from Calais.

Instant panic set in with Joelle. She hadn't had time to assess supplies at the house, much less get to the general store to fill in the gaps. And what about the sleeping arrangements? Were the linens clean or was that one other job she'd already fallen down on? She assumed at least one bedroom was suitable for habitation but they needed more than one.

William had immediately clued in to her distress and calmed her down by assuring her that her sisters were well aware of the living conditions and their only requirement was seeing her. Joelle appreciated

William's kind approach to her crisis, but that didn't solve the problem of upbringing, and Joelle's adoptive mother had been a real stickler for manners. No way could she allow people in her home—or what would be her home for the next two weeks—without attempting to be a good host.

They'd left the café and headed to the general store to see if Tyler was ready to leave. Even though William had already assured her she didn't need to provide anything for Alaina and Danae, Joelle picked up the best bottle of wine they had before hurrying out to jump in Tyler's truck.

Now she wished she would have bought crackers and dip—something to pick at while drinking the wine. Something to keep her hands busy while she had her first conversation with her sisters since they were all children.

Tyler looked over at her and frowned. "Are you nervous?"

Surprised that he'd even spoken, much less at the question, Joelle had to think a couple of seconds before responding.

"Yes," she finally admitted. "It's all a bit overwhelming and surreal. Not just that I will finally be reunited with my sisters—which I thought would never happen—but with everything that's happened surrounding our stepfather's death."

"I guess Dad filled you in on everything at lunch?"

"Probably not every detail, but I got the overview. As a social worker, I always think I've heard everything. Then occasionally, I'm still blown away at the things human beings will do to one another."

"I know exactly what you mean."

The sadness in his voice had her studying him for a moment, then she remembered—marine. "I guess you saw your share of horror overseas."

"We all did."

His speech was slightly abrupt, leaving her no doubt that his military service was something he didn't wish to talk about. Another piece of her softened toward him, because she understood that on a level that people who didn't deal every day with the horror of human behavior would never understand.

"I don't know why I'm so nervous about seeing my sisters again. I mean, I'm excited but also nervous."

He was silent for several seconds, and Joelle wondered if he'd even heard what she said. Or maybe he decided the conversation had gotten too girlie or too psychological.

"Maybe because you're afraid you won't fit with them," he said finally.

She stared at him, surprised at his intuitiveness. "Yes, I think you're right."

"Everyone needs to be where they belong— whether that's the place they live or a person they're with. But I don't think you have anything to worry about."

"No? Why is that? Have you met my sisters?"

"I haven't yet had the pleasure, but I've heard plenty about them from my dad. He thinks they're the best things since cable television came to Calais. My dad likes most people, but he admires few. No one has said anything yet, but I'm going to guess that he's planning on having Alaina take over his practice in Calais. She's already doing some work for him."

"Your dad is very sweet, but he also knew our mother, so it might make him a bit biased."

"Maybe, but Carter Trahan didn't know your mother. He's marrying Alaina and vouches for Danae. Carter and I have been friends since the crib, and trust me when I say a more shrewd human being has not been invented."

"I wish I would have gotten to the general store before he left. I'm looking forward to meeting him."

"He'll be keeping tabs on you for the estate, so I suppose you will soon enough."

Joelle held in a smile. Tyler was so direct and practical. On a normal day, she dealt with so much fabrication and drama that his what-you-see-is-what-you-get style was refreshing.

"So what do you plan on doing while we're conducting our Sisterhood Reunion?" she asked.

He frowned. "Staying out of the way."

His dismay was so comical that she couldn't hold in the laugh, but as he rounded the tree line and turned onto the circular drive in front of the house, she froze. The SUV in the driveway had a bumper sticker for a New England university. It had to be Alaina's car.

"They're here already," she said, her voice barely a whisper.

Tyler parked next to Alaina's vehicle. "I'm going to take a walk around the perimeter. I'll be around if you need me."

He jumped out of the truck and took off at a decent clip around the side of the house. Joelle's nervousness ticked up another notch as the only person she had any connection with fled. Not that she blamed him. It was an uncomfortable situation for her and she was one of the parties involved. Anyone else would feel even more uncomfortable, especially men, who, in her experience, tended to avoid questionable social situations anyway.

Grabbing the bottle of wine and her purse, she took a deep breath, then climbed out of the truck. The front door was open a crack, and she pushed it the rest of the way and stepped inside. Voices echoed down the kitchen hallway and she started that way. The voices sounded happy and excited, which helped her nerves a bit, but when she reached the threshold of the kitchen, she paused.

What if they hate me? What if I hate them?

She said a silent prayer, then stepped around the corner into the kitchen.

A tall, thin woman with long black hair pulled back in a ponytail stood in front of the refrigerator, her back to Joelle. A shorter, curvier woman with shoulder-length black hair stood at the counter, arranging cheese and crackers on a tray.

They were so busy chatting, they didn't hear her enter.

"Hello," she managed.

Immediately, all activity ceased and they both whirled around to stare at her. Joelle sucked in a breath as she looked at the tall woman.

Alaina.

She'd always looked like their mother. Joelle could remember that now. For a split second, all three of them held in that position, then they rushed over to her.

"Joelle," Alaina said as she stopped in front of Joelle, studying her face. "I remember now. You look like our father."

Alaina teared up and threw her arms around Joelle.

"I never thought I'd find you two," Alaina said. "It's a dream come true."

All of Joelle's nerves slipped away as she hugged Alaina. It all came flooding back to her—the love and admiration she'd always had for her big sister.

It was as if the years fell away and they were right back in step.

"My turn," Danae said, clapping her hands.

Alaina laughed as she released Joelle, who turned to look at a smiling Danae.

"The dimples," Joelle said. "I remember them."

Danae's smile widened and she wrapped her arms around Joelle, tightly squeezing her.

"I'm so glad William found you," Danae whispered.

"Me, too," Joelle said.

"This calls for a toast," Alaina said.

Danae released her and they both looked over at their big sister, who was pouring champagne into beautiful crystal glasses.

"I cleaned some of the crystal to get ready for this moment," Alaina said. "Please don't tell me you don't drink."

Joelle laughed. "I'm not a professional, but at the moment, I can't think of anything more perfect than champagne."

Alaina smiled and her whole face brightened, her happiness so clear. "You haven't had Danae's cheesecake yet. I bet it's more perfect than champagne, but she was cruel and wouldn't let me try a piece before we left."

Danae blushed a bit, clearly pleased with Alaina's praise, and Joelle felt her chest tighten as if her heart were expanding inside it. All the anxiety and doubts she'd felt were wasted emotion. These women were so comfortable...so right.

She took the glass of champagne that Alaina offered her and watched as Alaina lifted her glass in the air.

"To sisters," Alaina said. "To us."

"To us," Joelle and Danae repeated and they clinked their glasses together.

Joelle couldn't remember any moment in her life more perfect than this one.

TYLER MADE HIS way around the back of the house, pushing through the dense undergrowth, looking for any sign that someone else had passed this way recently. If Carter and his father both felt things weren't right on the LeBeau estate, then Tyler had no doubt they were right. If someone was prowling around the estate, he wanted to get a handle on it now and try to keep things from getting as out of hand as they had with Alaina and Danae.

So far, he'd turned up nothing. The house appeared tight as a drum. One window downstairs was broken, but it was boarded up. The rest were nailed shut. Danae's fiancé, Zach, the contractor making repairs to the house, had made sure everything was sealed tight before he returned to his regular workweek in New Orleans and so far, Tyler hadn't found a single thing the contractor had left undone.

Tyler knew the front door was the questionable point. It was a huge wooden double door, or-
nately carved, likely ridiculously expensive, and
was equipped with ancient hardware complete
with giant iron keys like those you'd see in a horror movie. In anticipation of Joelle's arrival, he'd
ordered some security equipment, but it hadn't
arrived until today. As soon as he finished his perimeter walk, he'd start setting up the equipment,
beginning with the alarm on the front door.

When he rounded the corner for the side of the
house containing the long patio, he paused, staring
into the brush. Something looked off. He stepped
into the trees and pushed through the foliage, working his way around a forty-foot-square region. On
the surface, everything appeared normal, but the
telltale signs of recent passage were visible to someone as skilled in tracking as Tyler was.

Some of the broken branches could be attributed
to the storms that had swept through the area lately,
but the depressions in the ground cover were the
result of being trod upon. The ground cover was
too dense to make out an actual footprint, but the
size of the indentations was too large for any of the
creatures that would normally roam the woods, except maybe bear. And if a bear had passed this way,
Tyler would see far more damage to the branches.

He followed the depressions and the broken
branches about twenty yards into the swamp be-

fore turning around. Someone could have traversed the swamp from any number of locations surrounding the house, and may have walked hundreds of yards or even miles to throw someone off the track. Likely, the tracks would come out on one of the many dirt paths that led through the swamp, easily reachable by an ATV. As most everyone in Calais owned or had access to an ATV, that didn't narrow the suspect pool even a bit.

Turning back, he tried to track the depressions toward the house, but they seemed to end about twenty feet from the patio, which made no sense. Tyler could understand if a stalker had a viewpoint to simply observe the comings and goings of the house in order to plan a strike. The military often watched from one vantage point but attacked from another. But from this vantage point, all he could see was the corner of the house and a bit of the patio. No window or door offered a view inside, except for the small pane of glass on the exterior door off the laundry room. But he couldn't see in that pane from his current position.

Deciding he wasn't going to figure it out standing there, he made a mental note to keep an eye on this location and continued back to the patio. The stone patio didn't leave any opportunity for tracks, so he checked the windows and scanned the nearby brush, but the only tracks he saw were his own from when he'd hauled away brush earlier that day.

As he made his way down the patio toward the kitchen, he heard the high-pitched voices of the three sisters. The excitement was clear in their tone, and Tyler was happy that Joelle's reunion with her sisters seemed to be going so well. He'd had no doubt that would be the case, but he understood why Joelle was nervous. It was a whole lot to absorb, especially some twenty-five years later and after living so long as an adult with no family to speak of.

He had a key to the patio door that led into the kitchen, but didn't want to startle them by letting himself in, so he rapped on the glass panes and waved when they whirled around. Joelle hurried to the door to let him in while her sisters stood there, clearly waiting for an introduction.

"Guys," Joelle said, "this is William's son, Tyler—my personal bodyguard."

They both smiled and the taller one walked over to extend her hand. "I should have known," she said. "You look just like your father. I'm Alaina."

"Nice to meet you," Tyler said. "You look like the pictures I've seen of your mother."

Alaina beamed and Tyler understood why his old friend Carter had gotten himself tied down. Alaina LeBeau was gorgeous and, according to his father, brilliant. And from limited exposure, he'd already gathered she had personality to boot. Triple threat. Carter had made a good choice.

"You must be Danae," he said and extended his hand to the youngest of Ophelia's daughters. Danae was shorter and curvier than Alaina, and looked like a combination of Alaina and Joelle. Perhaps she'd taken after both parents, while Joelle looked more like their father. Not that it mattered. Apparently any combination of those genes produced good-looking women.

Danae shook his hand and smiled. "It's nice to meet you. William talks so much about you. We're thrilled that you'll be checking up on Joelle. We worry about all of this, and it's too much for Carter to handle alone."

"Oh, he's not checking up," Joelle said. "He's living here, going with me when I leave the house. For all I know, he might be sitting guard outside the bathroom when I shower."

A flash of Joelle standing naked and wet under a shower stream bolted through his mind, and he felt his chest constrict. Instantly, he forced the image from his mind. The last thing he needed was to imagine Joelle—or any other woman—naked and vulnerable.

"I don't think it will come to that," he said. "Well, if you ladies are okay in here, I'm going to start installing a security alarm on the front door."

"That's a great idea," Alaina said.

Danae waved a hand over the counter, which was

loaded with food. "Do you want to eat? We brought a feast with us."

"Not right now, but I will take you up on that later if you don't mind."

"It's ready when you are," Danae said.

"Thank you for installing an alarm," Joelle said. "I know we'll all feel better sleeping here tonight."

Tyler gave them a nod and walked out of the kitchen.

"Stand outside the bathroom?" Alaina said. "I'd *totally* let him stand next to the shower and hold my towel."

They all laughed, then he heard Danae say, "You're awful. Entirely correct, but awful."

He smiled as he went to the entry to retrieve his equipment. Even the strongest man's ego couldn't ignore such compliments from beautiful women. He'd almost slowed for a moment, wondering if Joelle was going to comment, but decided it was information he didn't need.

Alaina and Danae were safe to admire. They were both attached to good men, but Joelle was risky. Granted, for all he knew, she could have a man back in Jackson, but he doubted it. She had a nervousness about her that seemed like a lack of recent socializing.

Maybe it's just me.

The thought crossed his mind and he frowned. True, he wasn't the most pleasant of people to be around, and he could have been a lot nicer when they'd met. He probably owed her an apology for his boorish behavior, but he wasn't likely to offer one. Less said, soonest mended was pretty much his motto.

He grabbed the box and removed the alarm. What he needed to do was focus on the job. Because he knew from firsthand experience what happened when he got sidetracked.

That was something he never intended to do again.

HE WATCHED THE house from the safety of the swamp. The women occupied the kitchen, clinking champagne glasses and eating hors d'oeuvres. They thought they had it all, but they were wrong. If it was the last thing he ever did, he was going to get what was coming to him. What he was due.

The man was somewhat of a concern. He had that posture that screamed military and a bulge at his waist that spelled concealed weapon. Right now, he could see the man, installing a security alarm on the front door.

What a waste of time.

Chapter Six

Joelle trailed up the enormous circular staircase with her sisters, studying every inch of the house, looking for something recognizable. When they reached the landing, she stopped short at the painting of her mother, directly in front of her. She took a hesitant step forward and touched the painting with her fingertips.

"This was here before," she said.

"You remember," Alaina said. "I didn't at first, but when Danae and I came across the picture tucked in one of the downstairs rooms, it came back to me. The painting hung here for as long as I can remember. The hook was still in the wall. So we dusted it off and put it back where it belongs."

Joelle looked over at Alaina. "You look so much like her. I remember being jealous of you, even at such a young age. Mother was the most beautiful woman I'd ever seen and I wanted to look like her, too."

Alaina smiled. "You were always wearing her

shoes. You'd find the highest set of heels in her closet and come shuffling down the hall. Mom was always afraid you'd fall and hurt yourself."

Joelle laughed. "She had a pair of shiny red ones that were my favorite."

Joelle turned back to the painting. "I remember this necklace." She ran a finger over the diamond necklace that circled her mother's neck. It had been her mother's prize piece and was always kept under lock and key.

"I wonder what happened to it," Joelle said.

Alaina shook her head. "I imagine Purcell sold it. Danae and I have poked into every area of the house. We've found some pretty things—some of them nice quality—but nothing of high value."

"But what about the art in the entry? Some of it looked valuable."

Alaina nodded. "I thought so, too, but upon closer examination, they appear to be reproductions. Good reproductions, but not near the value of the real thing. My guess is Purcell cleaned out anything that would bring him a fistful of cash."

"You're probably right." Joelle looked over at Danae, who wore a pensive look.

"Are you all right?" Joelle asked Danae.

"I'm fine," Danae assured her, but Joelle could tell something was bothering her.

"Danae doesn't remember," Alaina said quietly.

"Oh!" Joelle's heart went out to her sister, who

had been no more than a toddler when she was sent away.

"We're staying in our old bedroom," Alaina said. "It's the only room big enough for three beds and I didn't want us split up—not in this house. Danae…" Alaina looked over at Danae and bit her lower lip.

"I haven't gone in that room yet," Danae finished. "If I go in our room and don't remember anything, then I'm afraid I never will."

Joelle reached out and took Danae's hand in hers. "Then Alaina and I will remember for you."

Alaina took Danae's other hand in hers and nodded. "Absolutely."

Danae sniffed and smiled. "You guys are the best."

"We know," Alaina joked. "Now, let's go see that room."

They walked down the hall, hand in hand, until they reached the doorway. Alaina stepped inside first, then Joelle followed. A flood of recognition washed over her. The furniture was different, but the wallpaper was the same dusty-rose pattern that she remembered. In the corner sat the old wooden school desks that she'd spent hours at, coloring and learning her alphabet and numbers.

She looked back at Danae, who still lingered just outside the doorway. "It's okay," she said.

Her younger sister took a deep breath, then

closed her eyes and stepped inside the room. Joelle and Alaina each moved to her side and waited as she slowly let out the breath and opened her eyes. She scanned the room and Joelle could tell that nothing was clicking. Her heart broke for her little sister, who wanted so badly to remember.

Danae stepped away from them and walked over to the desks. She lifted the top of the first desk and pulled out a pink plastic comb. Suddenly, she spun around, her eyes wide with excitement.

"Mom used to comb our hair with this." A single tear fell down her cheek. "It's faint—almost like I dreamed it—but I remember. I remember."

Joelle's heart was practically bursting with happiness for her little sister. On the surface, it didn't seem like a lot, but Joelle understood how monumental it was for Danae. She stepped over beside her and ran one hand over the scarred desktop.

"I wonder how many hours we spent at these desks," Joelle said to Alaina.

"Hundreds," Alaina replied. "Thousands, maybe."

A memory, so vivid it seemed like a movie running through her mind, came to Joelle in a flash. She squatted down and reached underneath the seat. She didn't expect to find anything but an empty cubbyhole, and when her fingers brushed against soft velvet, she gasped.

"What?" Alaina asked. Her eyes widened. "No. It's still there?"

Danae stared down at the purple bag in Joelle's hands. "That's a Crown Royal bag. Were you two child alkies?"

Joelle laughed. "No, but we loved purple and we begged for the bag. Mom said no for so long, which I totally get now, but it made no sense then."

"We harassed her," Alaina agreed. "Open it."

Joelle pulled the drawstring on the bag and turned it over. Gray rocks tumbled out onto her palm.

"Rocks?" Danae raised her eyebrows.

"Joelle loved to play in the dirt in the driveway," Alaina said, her eyes bright with the memory. "We built roads and forts and fences for our plastic ponies."

"Purcell hated it," Joelle said. "He thought little girls should sit silently and be pretty, not play in dirt, and especially not track it inside."

"But Mom didn't care, and let us do it anyway," Alaina said. "One time Joelle got sick—I don't remember with what—and she had to stay in bed. It was beautiful weather and she was so mad that she couldn't go outside with me. Mom and I went outside and picked up rocks. She told me to hide them in my pockets so that Purcell wouldn't see. Then we hurried upstairs and she pulled out the purple bag to put the rocks in for Joelle."

"She told us to keep the bag and the rocks hidden so we wouldn't get in trouble for having either of them," Joelle said. "We played with them all day, and then I hid them in the cubbyhole. I'd completely forgotten."

"You were well enough to go outside the next day," Alaina said. "So it was business as usual."

Danae smiled. "I know I'll never remember things like the two of you, but I'm so glad you're here to tell me about them. The way you describe things, I can picture them in my mind."

Alaina sniffed. "It seems so strange to me, that I had almost no memory of this place when I first returned, but the longer I'm in Calais, the more I remember. I don't know why I'd forgotten so much."

Joelle glanced at Alaina, who gazed around the room. She wondered, too, why Alaina had no memories before. Being two years older, Alaina should have more memories than Joelle, not fewer. If Joelle had to guess, something had caused Alaina to shut her childhood off—to compartmentalize it and file it away where she didn't access it. In Joelle's line of work, she saw a lot of that, but usually only following a great trauma.

Joelle couldn't help but wonder if Alaina would ever remember the thing or things that prevented her from clear recall.

Alaina reached for Danae's hand and gave it a squeeze. "I promise I'll share everything with you. More of the past returns to me every day."

Joelle froze for a moment, then recovered. Certainly, she wanted to share with her sisters, but she wasn't ready to share everything. Not yet. Not until she knew more about her mother and Purcell, and not until she had a better idea why Alaina couldn't remember more.

Joelle stepped over toward the closet and ran her fingers across three holes in the wall, remembering what William had told her about Alaina's attacker.

"Bullet holes," Alaina answered her unspoken question.

Joelle spun around. "Are you okay to stay in here?"

Alaina nodded. "It's our room…our house. I want us to reclaim everything. This seemed like the best place to start."

"Then I say we haul the champagne up here and christen it."

Alaina smiled. "Sounds like a plan."

They hurried back down to the kitchen to re-fill their glasses. As Alaina poured, Joelle's cell phone buzzed. She frowned as she reached for her purse and pulled out the phone. She had a text message, but not from a number she recognized. She punched the button to read the text and gasped.

Give me what's mine.

Her fingers tightened on the phone so hard they hurt. It couldn't be.

"What's wrong?" Danae asked.

"It's nothing," Joelle said, not about to let Victor Brant spoil their night.

Danae glanced over at Alaina, who raised her eyebrows. Clearly, neither of her sisters believed her for a moment.

"You may as well give up trying to keep things from us," Alaina said. "Danae is as street-smart as they come, and I've made witnesses cry in the courtroom. You're not going to get anything past either of us."

"You shouldn't even try," Danae said. "You're our sister. Your problems are our problems."

Joelle looked at both their faces and sighed. If they were anywhere near as stubborn as she was, they weren't going to let this go. She may as well tell them and get it over with.

"There was an incident before I left Jackson," Joelle said, then told them about Brant and his threats.

"Why haven't the police picked him up?" Alaina asked.

"Because I can't prove it was him, but I know it was, if that makes any sense."

Danae nodded. "Makes perfect sense. So do you think this Brant is capable of destroying more than a car?"

"No one can ever be certain, but if I had to guess, then I'd say yes. That's why I agreed to come right away. I talked it over with my boss and the Jackson police, and everyone felt my leaving town would give him time to cool off."

"Does he know where you are?"

"No. Only my boss and the Jackson police know. I didn't tell anyone else." She frowned. "This is a new phone. Only my boss, the police, you two and William have the number. How did he get it so quickly?"

"I assume it's unlisted?" Alaina asked.

"Yeah. In my line of work, that's the norm."

"Carter will be by here soon," Alaina said. "You need to tell him about this…about everything."

"He's bluffing," Joelle argued. "He doesn't even know where I am. How could he come after me?"

"He got your phone number," Alaina said. "If he could get that, he could get the rest."

IT WAS ALMOST dawn when more glasses of champagne and soda than Joelle could count sent her shuffling down the hall to the bathroom. She and her sisters had sat up in the bedroom, talking through the wee hours of the morning until none of them could stay awake any longer. Carter had been and gone hours before, promising to follow up with the Jackson police and to let her know the next morning what their thoughts were.

Tyler had taken everything in when she'd explained the situation to Carter, but hadn't said a word. Then the two men had spoken for some time outside at Carter's truck, and Joelle had no doubt they were comparing notes and formulating a plan to keep the womenfolk safe. At any other time, the feminist in her might have found it annoying, but the genuine concern kept her from feeling anything but grateful that such capable men had her back.

Wincing as a floorboard creaked, she glanced at the bedroom where Tyler was staying. It had unnerved her a bit that a mere wall would separate them, but he wanted to be in hearing distance, just in case. The door was pulled mostly shut, leaving only a thin crack with moonlight streaming through it.

She was almost to the bathroom when her foot brushed across something hard and cold. The dim glow from the entry lights illuminated the balcony, and she could see something shiny on the floor. As she bent over to pick it up, she realized it was a quarter. She clasped her fingers around it and looked up before straightening. From that position, she could see through the balcony banisters down into the massive entry.

A flash of pain came over her and in an instant, twenty-five years slipped away.

MOMMY WAS CRYING *again. She cried a lot since the bad man came. He'd married Mommy but he wasn't Daddy. Daddy was in heaven with the angels, but Joelle wished he would come back. Mommy and her and her sisters needed him more than the angels did.*

The bad man yelled at Mommy again and Joelle ducked lower, clutching the banisters with her small hands. If the bad man saw her, he'd spank her like he did last time he caught her watching them. Spying, he called it, but Joelle didn't know what spying meant.

She wondered for a moment if she should go get Alaina. Her older sister hated when she woke her up in the middle of the night, but she wouldn't mind being awakened if it was to protect Mommy. Alaina was older. She would know what to do.

As she gripped the banisters and started to rise, the bad man raised his hand and slapped Mommy across the face. Unable to help herself, she cried out, telling Mommy to run. Instantly, the bad man whipped around and pinned his gaze on her. She knew she should run but she was frozen in place, as if nailed to the floor.

The bad man started toward the stairs, but Mommy grabbed his arm, trying to prevent him from going after her. He pushed Mommy and she crashed down on the floor. Joelle sprang up from the balcony and ran to the bedroom, locking the door behind her like Mommy had taught her and Alaina to do.

She ran across the floor and jumped into her bed, pulling the covers up over her head. The bad man's footsteps echoed in the hallway outside of their room. She lowered the covers just enough to see the door. The doorknob jiggled and she heard the bad man say a curse word.

Joelle clenched the covers tighter, and wondered why Alaina didn't hear the bad man—why she didn't wake up and tell Joelle what to do. It seemed like forever, but finally the jiggling stopped and she heard the bad man stomping away from their room. When she couldn't hear his footsteps any longer, she grabbed her blanket and crawled under her bed, where she remained the rest of the night.

JOELLE BOLTED UP so quickly, she staggered backward. When her hands met with the wall, she leaned back against it, trying to catch her breath. Her heart pounded in her temples and her chest ached with every rise and fall.

She'd had the visions as long as she could remember, but never had she had one that played out at such length and in such detail. Never had she remembered her stepfather coming after her, or her sleeping under her bed. Never had one of the visions brought the sheer panic she now felt—anger, certainly, but never panic.

She pushed herself off the wall, knowing that it would be no use to attempt to go back to sleep. Maybe she'd finish up in the bathroom and head downstairs to make coffee. As she reached for the bathroom door, a squeaking sound carried from downstairs. Immediately, she froze. It had sounded like a door opening, but surely she was mistaken. The front door had an alarm and all the other doors had new locks that Carter had installed. There was no longer any chance that random Calais residents were wandering around with keys to the other doors, as Alaina and Danae told her had happened when they first got to town.

Deciding she must have been mistaken, she pushed the bathroom door open and that's when she heard the squeaking sound again—this time louder.

Before she could even think about waking Tyler, he rushed out of his bedroom and ran straight into her, knocking her to the floor. It only took him a second to realize whom he'd crashed into, then he cursed and hauled her up from the floor the same way he'd pulled her out of the brush the day before.

The girls' bedroom door flew open and Alaina and Danae bolted into the hall, both clutching pistols. Tyler took one look at them and raised his eyebrows.

"I'm not sure whether to be impressed or afraid," he said.

"Definitely afraid," Alaina said as they lowered their weapons. "What happened?"

"I heard a noise," Tyler said, "and rushed out to

investigate, but only managed to tackle your sister. Was it you who made the noise?"

"No," Joelle said. "I was just about to wake you. It came from downstairs. I dismissed it as an old house creaking the first time, but the second time, I'm certain it was a door opening or closing."

Tyler cursed again, then ran downstairs, and it was only then that Joelle realized he had a nine millimeter in his hand.

"Unbelievable," Joelle said. "I'm the only one in this house who doesn't sleep with their hand on a loaded gun. And I'm the social worker."

"This house," Danae said, "is *why* we sleep with our hands on loaded guns."

"Should we go after him?" Alaina asked.

"He probably won't appreciate it if we do," Danae said, "but that's not going to stop me."

Danae took off after Tyler with Alaina only a step behind. Joelle stared after them for a moment, then ran to catch up. At the bottom of the stairs, they peered into the dim light, trying to figure out which direction Tyler had gone, but there was no movement or noise to guide them.

Just as Joelle was going to suggest they call for him, the light in the kitchen came on, illuminating the hallway. Alaina motioned to Joelle to get behind her, and she and Danae lifted their pistols and walked down the hallway.

"Stop!" Tyler's voice boomed from the kitchen when they reached the archway.

Alaina stopped short and Joelle had to grab her shoulders to keep from running into her.

"What's wrong?" Alaina asked.

"I don't want you to ruin evidence," Tyler said.

Alaina's eyes narrowed and Joelle knew her sister had slipped into attorney mode. She'd seen that look so many times in court.

"What evidence?" Alaina asked.

"I'm not sure yet, but I rigged the downstairs after you guys went to bed. I wanted to get to the bottom of things."

"Rigged how?" Joelle asked.

"I sprinkled powder across some thresholds and in front of exterior doors."

Danae nodded. "To see if someone passed there. Smart."

"And someone passed through the kitchen?" Alaina asked.

Tyler squatted down and inspected the floor in front of them. Joelle could barely make out the fine powder scattered on the stone tile.

"It doesn't look like anyone passed this way," he said, "or through the patio door."

"What about the door off the laundry room?" Alaina asked.

"I was going to check there next," he said.

"We'll come with you," Danae said.

He paused and Joelle knew he wanted to tell them to stay put, but he was far too smart to argue with three angry women, two of whom were toting guns.

"Hurry up, then," he said as he rushed past them and back to the entry.

The laundry room was at the end of a hallway off the back of the huge entry. It took ten seconds to get there and only one glance at the floor to see that Tyler's trap had worked. Right in front of the exterior door was a single footprint, stamped in powder.

The dead bolt was pulled back in the open position. Tyler turned the doorknob and pulled the door open. Joelle sucked in a breath. "He left through this door, but how did he get in?"

Tyler closed the door, locked it and pulled the dead bolt back into place. The frustration he felt rolled off of him.

"I don't know, but you can bet I'm going to find out."

Chapter Seven

Gray, gloomy skies presided over the cemetery in New Orleans where Tyler stood with his father, Carter, Joelle, Alaina, Danae and her fiancé, Zach, waiting for the medical examiner to direct his staff to open the LeBeau family crypt and remove Ophelia LeBeau's coffin. William had already provided the key to the crypt, courtesy of the LeBeau estate attorney's office in New Orleans.

Tyler stood back a bit from the rest of them, wishing things had not come down to this—wishing the sisters had chosen to leave the exhumation to professionals used to dealing with such sordid things and not chosen to stand there, waiting. Their first glimpse of their mother, after twenty-five years, was going to be shocking, and despite the fact that they were all strong, intelligent women, Tyler didn't think they were ready for it.

The medical examiner opened the crypt and directed his staff to the correct vault box. Tyler could see the assistants pulling the coffin out of the box inside and noticed that the sisters shifted so that they stood close together. As the assistants carried the coffin out of the crypt, it started to mist.

The medical examiner had come prepared for such a disruption and directed his staff to the easy-up tent placed to the side of the crypt. The staff placed the coffin on the ground under the tent, then stepped back so that the medical examiner could take over. He pulled on a mask and stepped up to the coffin, placing a crowbar under the lip. One of the assistants moved into position behind him, ready to take the required pictures to document the exhumation prior to transport.

He saw the sisters take one another's hands and looked over at Carter, who glanced back at him, the worry on his face clear as day. Prior to returning to Calais, Carter had been a homicide detective with the New Orleans Police Department. He'd seen bodies in various states of decay. In the Middle East, Tyler had seen every possible atrocity one could imagine and many one couldn't stretch the mind to think of.

But these three women hadn't seen anything like what the two of them had.

Tyler watched Joelle as the medical examiner clenched the crowbar, preparing to open the coffin. He shoved the crowbar down and the wood splintered, a loud crack echoing across the cemetery. Joelle winced and swallowed, but all three girls held fast. The medical examiner set the crowbar on the ground and reached out one gloved hand to lift the coffin lid.

Everyone leaned forward except Tyler, who had returned to Calais to avoid exactly this kind of sight. Instead of looking at the coffin, Tyler watched Joelle—the only sister without a fiancé—ready to be by her side in a second if she needed him.

He heard the sound of the coffin lid slamming back, and then everyone gasped. Joelle threw her hand over her mouth and stumbled backward into Tyler, who clutched her shoulders to steady her and peered over to see if anything was out of the ordinary.

What he saw was an empty box.

EVERYONE BUT THE medical examiner and his staff was crowded inside Zach and Danae's one-bedroom condo in New Orleans. Joelle stood near the fireplace, looking at framed pictures of Zach and Danae. The smiling Zach in the photos looked completely different from the shaken and pale Zach they'd brought home. Joelle didn't understand why Danae's fiancé had taken this so hard, but it was something she'd ask Alaina about later.

The bedroom door opened and William, who'd been inside with Danae and Zach, stepped out.

"Are they okay?" Alaina asked.

"They're fine. Zach is understandably upset, and

Danae is trying to reassure him that none of this casts light on him."

Joelle frowned. "I don't understand."

William nodded and walked over to stand beside her. "I didn't have time to cover all the details in our meeting the other day, but our friend Zach came to Calais looking for answers of his own. His father was the funeral director that your stepfather paid off. He attempted a deathbed confession but all Zach understood was your mother's name."

"Oh!" The implications of everything William said rolled over Joelle like a tidal wave. "But Zach didn't have anything to do with that. He's as much a victim of Purcell's actions as we all are."

William smiled and gave her arm a squeeze. "Of course he is, but he can't help feeling responsible on some level. After all, his father was part of something that hurt the woman he loves. Don't worry about Zach. He just needs some time to process all of this, and seeing you all is harder at the moment."

"We should go," Tyler said. "Give him some space."

Alaina nodded. "I'll just tell Danae we're going." She slipped into the bedroom and was back out a minute later.

"Danae said to tell everyone thank you and that they'll be in Calais this weekend," Alaina said.

William, who'd ridden to New Orleans with Tyler and Joelle, looked over at Carter. "If it's all right,

I'd like to ride back to Calais with you so that we can discuss what needs to happen next, from a law enforcement and legal perspective."

"Of course," Carter said.

Joelle trailed out of the building, not entirely comfortable with spending the two-hour drive alone in the truck with Tyler. Although he'd been pleasant enough the night before when the girls had their sleepover, he'd gone right back to silent and closed off after discovering evidence of the intruder. He'd remained silent through the entire exhumation process, and Joelle didn't relish the long, boring, uncomfortable drive.

The first twenty minutes passed in exactly the manner Joelle expected—she tried not to fidget and Tyler stared straight out the windshield, not saying a word.

Finally, he looked over at her. "Are you all right?"

"Yes. Your truck is quite comfortable—almost like riding on my couch."

She could see a smile hovering around his lips, but it didn't quite break through.

"Thank you," he said, "but that's not what I meant. I'm talking about the exhumation."

"Oh, well," she said, trying to formulate a good response to a question she hadn't yet answered for herself. "I'm all right, but I don't know what I think about it."

"You've had an awful lot to wrap your mind around in a short amount of time."

"True, but at least I have the education and experience to handle crisis. I can't imagine what your average person would do in my situation."

"Sit in a corner crying or run screaming from the town, is my guess."

"I've actually considered both, but neither seemed overly productive."

Now the smile broke through. "I tell you what— I give all you ladies credit for being tough. When your sisters ran out of the bedroom last night, wearing pink pajamas and packing guns, it gave me a bit of a start. Then the more I thought about it, the bigger kick I got out of it."

"I got a kick out of it, too. It's nice to know my sisters *really* have my back."

"Did anything else happen...before you heard the noise?"

Joelle stiffened, somewhat taken aback. "No," she lied. "Why do you ask?"

He shrugged. "You were pale and your hands were shaking as if you'd had a recent shock."

Instantly, Joelle's mind leaped back to the vision she'd seen looking through the banisters. Tyler was far more perceptive than she'd given him credit for if he'd picked up on her reaction. But no matter how pleasant things seemed at the moment with the hunky bodyguard, her childhood flashbacks were something she wasn't ready to share with any-one—not even her sisters.

"I think I was just unnerved," she said finally. "You know, big spooky house…things that go bump in the night…and after hearing everything that happened to Alaina and Danae, I suppose my imagination is working overtime."

"Hmm," he said, but didn't look the least bit convinced.

She looked out the windshield, mentally running through the morning's events. "What do you think it means?"

"The empty casket?"

"Yeah. The medical examiner was quite clear on the fact that the casket had never been opened. So it's not like Purcell could have sent someone to steal the body after the fact. And since the serial number inside the casket matched the burial records, I don't see how the entire casket could have been switched."

"Unless someone made up plates for the replacement casket that matched the records, or switched the casket before the burial."

"But why?" she asked. "She was going in the crypt. No one suspected foul play. Why take such a risk?"

"Just to be certain that nothing could ever be traced back to him? Honestly, I don't know. Purcell was a hit man for a mob family. It's hard for a person with morals to get into that mind-set."

"But Carter is trying to."

Tyler nodded. "Carter takes his job seriously, and with you three involved, it's personal. He won't give up—no matter how long it takes."

"You trust him," Joelle said, a bit surprised that the cagey bodyguard had such absolute faith in someone other than himself.

"I've known Carter my whole life. Him, his mother and my father—I've never seen any of them do or say something without someone else in mind. Carter would never talk about it, because he'd consider it bragging and therefore rude, but my dad told me he received several commendations when he was a detective in New Orleans."

"Then it looks like I'm well protected. Your father told me you have quite a collection of medals yourself."

Immediately, Tyler stiffened and his jaw flexed. "My dad shouldn't talk about things he doesn't understand."

Even though she knew she'd hit a nerve, Joelle couldn't help saying, "He's proud of you."

Tyler stared out the windshield for several seconds before responding. "Maybe I'm not proud of some of the things those medals were given for."

Joelle stared at him, his words hitting her like a tidal wave. It was easy to watch the news footage from the Middle East on the television and shake your head, but had she ever once thought about the extent of mental and emotional damage that was inflicted on those simply doing their job?

In her own work, she'd done things during crisis situations that she would never have done under normal circumstances. She'd hit people, broken major traffic laws and effectively kidnapped children to remove them from dangerous situations. She'd never regretted a single action she'd taken to save a woman or a child, but sometimes the extent of her anger during the fray disturbed her. It gave her a clear understanding of how much humans were capable of when placed in volatile situations.

Given Tyler's length of time overseas, the things he'd seen probably made a day at her job look like Disneyland.

And she'd just opened her big mouth and brought it all back to the forefront of his mind.

Idiot.

She slumped back against the truck seat and focused her mind on the first project she intended to work on at the house. Every time she opened her mouth, she made things between her and Tyler more uncomfortable. Maybe it was time to be quiet.

Chapter Eight

Tyler managed to endure the rest of the drive to the mansion in calm silence but it was a strain. Why had his dad brought up his medals? Tyler understood that William was proud of him, but the last thing he wanted people doing was thinking him a hero, when he knew the truth. And the very last person he needed thinking him a hero was a woman with a dangerous job and living in a dangerous situation.

He'd already played that game and lost.

From now on, no more personal conversations with Joelle. He'd be polite, but no one claimed being buddies with her was part of the job he was hired to do. Talking to her always brought him back around to things he'd come back to Calais to forget.

He checked all the windows and doors in the house as soon as they arrived, then went back outside to do another perimeter search, desperately needing to work off some pent-up energy. Also, he was determined to discover how the intruder had gained access to the house. If he couldn't prevent access to the structure, how was he supposed to protect Joelle? The last thing he needed was something to happen to the heiress on his watch.

As he walked around the side of the house, scanning the ground for any trace of recent passage besides his own, his mind rolled through the conversation they'd had on the ride back from New Orleans. When he'd run out of his bedroom the night before, something had startled Joelle. Something besides the noise she heard downstairs.

The expression on her face went far beyond simple fear and crossed right into haunted. He'd seen that look on so many soldiers—young men who weren't prepared well for the atrocities they would face or the things they'd be asked to do. Joelle had seen or heard something that forced her to remember something particularly horrible. So horrible she couldn't control her body's reaction to it and refused to discuss it.

Alaina is starting to remember more....

Something his dad said during a recent discussion ran through Tyler's mind. William had said that despite being the oldest of the sisters, Alaina didn't have much memory of her childhood at the LeBeau estate. William thought she'd blocked it out because the death of her mother and being sent to live with strangers was so traumatic for a six-year-old girl. But since returning to Calais, Alaina's memory was starting to return, and Carter hoped that at some point, her memories might help them unravel what happened to her mother.

Joelle was only four when she was sent away, but even someone so young could have memories, if they had produced great emotion. Overwhelming happiness and extreme fear would be enough to imprint on a four-year-old. Based on Joelle's expression when he came out of his bedroom, he was betting on fear.

The question was, were the memories always present, or like Alaina, had something come flooding back since she'd returned to the house?

Either way, she'd clammed up as soon as he asked. Maybe he'd mention his suspicions to Carter, who would tell Alaina. Perhaps if Joelle knew her sister was remembering, she'd be willing to tell her secrets to Alaina.

As he rounded the corner to the patio side of the house, he looked into the swamp toward the clearing he'd seen the day before. Dark clouds were starting to form overhead, and he knew he had little daylight left before the rain began, so he stepped into the swamp to see if he could discern any more details of passage.

At the edge of the clearing, he hit pay dirt. Where leaves had been the day before, now a patch of loose dirt remained, and at the edge of it was the front half of a shoe print. Without making a cast, there was no way to be certain, but it looked like the same size and shape as the print he'd lifted from the laundry room.

He followed the trail into the swamp for about a hundred yards before stopping. It wasn't safe to leave Joelle unprotected. He'd wait until Carter was available to keep watch, then he'd track the intruder to his getaway point. It probably wouldn't tell them who the intruder was, but it would be one more thing in their arsenal of knowledge.

As soon as he got back inside, and if he had any service left on his phone with the storm moving in, he'd order outdoor video cameras with motion detectors. Someone had used this path twice that he knew of. He'd stopped at a supply store in New Orleans on the way to the cemetery and picked up some cameras to place inside the house. Maybe if he didn't catch them inside, he could catch them outside. Either way, a picture or video would put the entire thing to rest, quickly and easily.

He headed back to the house and as he stepped on the patio, his cell phone rang. It was Carter, so he answered, happy service hadn't dropped yet.

"I'm glad I caught you," Carter said. "With the storm coming, I didn't figure I would."

"I expect service will go anytime now. What's up?"

"I talked with the Jackson police. Brant is MIA.

He left his house three days ago and no one has seen or heard from him since."

"That's not good."

"It gets worse. The Jackson police ran his credit cards and one of them was used last night at a hotel and restaurant in New Orleans."

Tyler cursed. "And I suppose there's no legitimate reason for him to be in New Orleans?"

"No family or friends, and his secretary says they don't have any business interests or contacts in New Orleans that he would need to see. Besides, if it was legitimate, his secretary would know where he was. She's been trying to reach him for two days with no luck."

"Have the police tried triangulating his cell phone?"

"Not yet, but I asked them to. They're supposed to call me when they get something."

"Good, let me know."

Tyler waited several seconds, but no response was forthcoming. Then his phone beeped twice and he looked at the display and sighed. No service. And he hadn't gotten a chance to tell Carter about his theory on Joelle's childhood memories.

He glanced overhead and saw that the clouds had almost covered the sky and grew darker by the second. He needed to finish his outside rounds and get inside. Ordering the night-vision cameras would have to wait until the next day. The rain wasn't supposed to clear out until the next evening, but his dad had Wi-Fi, and if he headed into town early enough, he could probably catch Carter at the café.

He worked his way down the patio, but didn't see anything out of place, then let himself in the patio door and into the kitchen. Joelle was nowhere in sight, so he figured she was upstairs. He started across the kitchen when suddenly, the pantry door flew open.

If his reflexes had been any slower, it would have smacked him directly in the face, but he got his hand up in time to stop it.

"Oh!" Joelle cried out as she stepped around the door. "I'm so sorry. I didn't know you were there."

He struggled to control his aggravation. "What are you doing hiding in the pantry?"

"It's not a pantry. Well, at least, not like any I've ever seen. See?"

She pushed the door completely open and he peered inside. Joelle was right. It wasn't like any pantry he'd ever seen, either. It was approximately eight feet wide and at least ten feet long. Shelves lined one wall from top to bottom. On the other side rested cabinets with a stone countertop as well as another set of countertops above. At the opposite side of the pantry was another door.

"Where does that go?" he asked.

Joelle stepped through the pantry and opened the other door. "It's filled with junk now, but with that chandelier, I'm going to guess this was the formal dining room. I think that's a butler's pantry."

"What the heck is a butler's pantry?"

"Wealthy people often had a room connecting the kitchen to the formal dining that the staff could use to prepare the food for service. That way they didn't walk up and down the main halls of the home carrying trays."

"Like the servants' stairs that lead from the upstairs directly to the kitchen and the laundry room?"

"Exactly. The premise was that the servants' work should be visible everywhere, but not the people themselves."

"Sounds like a lot of pompous nonsense to me."

"My great-grandparents—or maybe even someone before that—built the house. My guess is it's what they were used to. But I agree with you, it seems an odd way to live—with people roaming your house all the time."

"You don't remember servants from when you lived here before?" Tyler asked, hoping to get some idea of the extent of Joelle's childhood memories.

Joelle frowned and she shifted her glance down before answering. "I don't really remember much. I think I was too young."

"Really? It seems like something should register, even at four. You don't even remember your mother?"

Her face softened a bit and she nodded. "Sometimes, but it's not clear. More like glancing at a photograph or a tiny video clip. It's usually gone as quickly as it appeared."

"Carter said Alaina started to remember things after she returned to the house."

"That's what she said the other night. I did remember a couple of things when I walked into our old room, but it was still like the others—snatches of the past."

Tyler studied her closely, but she appeared to be telling the truth. "Carter said he's hoping that Alaina will remember something that can help him with the investigation."

Her eyes widened. "Really? I don't see how…"

"For instance, we know your stepfather paid off people—it's possible Alaina could have seen some of those people meeting with him. If she remembers anyone we haven't already identified, it might help us figure out who's still accessing the house and why."

"Oh. I'd never thought of it that way, but it still seems such a long shot, a child that young being able to not only remember a face but extrapolate it to that person now."

"You work with kids who've been through traumatic experiences a lot," Tyler continued to push. "Surely you've seen cases where they saw something so bad that they pushed it to the back of their mind, only to have it resurface later on."

She frowned. "And you think Alaina might have seen something so bad that she blocked all her memories of her childhood here?"

Tyler shrugged. "I'm no psychologist. You'd be able to answer that question better than me."

She was silent for a couple of seconds, and he could tell she was trying to formulate a response. Finally, she put her hands up in the air and said, "It's certainly possible, but I can't say whether it's something Alaina is experiencing. At least, she hasn't said so to me."

She glanced out the window at the dark clouds. "I guess I better go to the laundry room and get the lanterns and flashlights that Alaina told me about."

Tyler watched her as she hurried out of the room. He hadn't been mistaken. For just a millisecond, that same haunted expression he'd seen on her face the night before had flashed by. If he hadn't been watching closely for it, he would have missed it entirely.

Alaina may not be experiencing a recollection of something traumatic, but he'd bet any amount of money that Joelle was.

CARTER TOSSED HIS cell phone on the kitchen counter and looked over at Alaina, who was spooning chicken gumbo into two bowls.

"No service?" she asked.

"I've got service on this end, but my guess is

there's none left at the house. Not with this storm moving in."

Alaina nodded. "I had my share of that problem. I wish we could have gotten a landline installed before Joelle came, but William said it would take months. She didn't want to wait, but I wish she had."

Carter took the bowls of gumbo from Alaina and placed them on the breakfast table. "My guess is Joelle wanted to get away from Brant. It's a smart thing to do—leave town for a couple of weeks and give him a chance to cool off and wise up."

Alaina set two glasses of tea on the table. "Except that it doesn't appear he's done either."

"No," Carter said, still unhappy over the Jackson Police Department's report on Brant. "Well, if he makes the mistake of coming to Calais, we'll be ready for him. First thing tomorrow, I'll circulate a picture of him to every businessman and otherwise sane individual in Calais. If anyone sees him, they'll let me know."

"Someone from the outside can still get to you," Alaina said quietly.

Carter wrapped his arms around his wife and kissed the top of her head. "In your case, we didn't know we were looking for an outsider, much less who he was. Joelle's situation is different."

Alaina leaned back and looked up at him. "Is it? Someone's still gaining access to the house, and

I seriously doubt that's Brant. Not this soon, and not without avoiding detection. Whoever is entering that house has an agenda and a way in we've yet to figure out. And that means Joelle is in just as much danger as Danae and I were."

"We're better prepared this time," Carter assured her. "We know he's out there. We know some of what happened and we're uncovering more every week. And Tyler's there. She's got full-time, on-site, ridiculously qualified security, *and* I trust him."

Alaina studied his face for a moment, still not appearing convinced, but finally she nodded. "I know you're doing everything you can, and because Tyler is William's son, I trust him, too, even though I don't know him that well."

"But?"

She blew out a breath. "But after today, I just don't know what to think anymore. I'm starting to think that we've only scratched the surface of my stepfather's sins."

"You may be right."

Alaina's eyes misted up and she sniffed. "What did he do to her, Carter? Where is my mother's body?"

Carter pulled his fiancé to his chest and hugged her tightly. "I don't know, but I'm going to find out. If it's the last thing I ever do."

Chapter Nine

Joelle set the lantern on the nightstand next to the twin bed she'd claimed as hers the night before. Rain had been falling steadily for a couple of hours, but apparently, it hadn't gotten bad enough to cut off power. Still, having the lantern in easy reach made her feel better.

After fleeing from Tyler and his questions, she'd gathered bad-weather supplies, then spent the rest of the evening wandering from room to room, digging through the contents, and marveling over the beautiful art and paintings shoved in piles, boxes and closets. According to Alaina, most of it probably wasn't worth much, but some of it looked fantastic. If her sisters didn't mind, Joelle intended to ask if she could keep a couple of the items. She would purchase them, if needed.

She'd found a particularly lovely painting of Alaina as a baby tucked behind a buffet table in the formal dining room. Even though she couldn't have been any older than six months in the portrait, Alaina already favored their mother. Joelle had eased the painting out from behind the buffet and leaned it against the door to the butler's pantry. As soon as she got an opportunity, she'd inquire about getting the piece professionally cleaned.

Tyler had gone back into silent mode and had spent the entire evening installing motion-activated cameras around the house. With no wireless internet available, he had to hard-wire the devices. Joelle had heard a lot of mumbling as he tried to decide where the wire would be least visible. As she didn't have the skill set to offer any aid, she went quietly about her business and tried to stay out of his way.

After several dust-filled hours, she'd finally stopped poking through things, and her thoughts turned to a long overdue shower. She was on her way down the hall to the bathroom when she heard a knock at the front door. Frowning, she glanced at her watch. Seven o'clock. The storm and the gloomy house made it feel later than it was, but still, who would be out in the middle of the swamp in a storm?

She hurried down the stairs and arrived at the front door the same time as Tyler, who'd come from the kitchen.

"Wait," he said and pulled out his pistol. He opened the door a crack and peered outside, then opened it wide and motioned someone inside.

The man was on crutches and looked to be a

hundred years old. He pulled back the hood of his rain slicker and looked straight at Joelle. Tyler must know the man if he'd let him inside the house, so she gave him a polite smile. Then something in her clicked.

"Amos," she whispered. "Is it really you?"

The old man broke out in a grin. "You remember?"

Given the crutches and his obvious frailty, she was afraid to hug him, but she leaned over and gave the old caretaker a kiss on the cheek. "Of course I remember. You had all those wonderful tools."

"You liked my nail gun the best, but your mother wouldn't let you use it. You pitched a righteous fit over it, if I remember correct."

Joelle smiled. "I'm sure your memory is fine, although I don't relish recalling any of my somewhat spoiled behavior. Please come into the kitchen and sit."

"Can't right now. My niece is out front waiting to take me to a cousin's in New Orleans. I have a doctor's appointment tomorrow so they can check my foot. They're thinking they might have to reset it, so I might be gone a couple more days. But I promise you, when I get back, we'll sit down and have us a chat."

"I'm looking forward to it," Joelle said. "Take care, Amos, and thank you so much for dropping by."

Joelle watched as the caretaker navigated the

stone driveway and hopped into a sedan, then Tyler closed the door and drew the dead bolt into place.

"He seemed ancient when I was a child. I can't believe he's still alive," Joelle said. "How old is he?"

"I'm not sure even Amos knows, but my dad says he has to be in his eighties at least."

"He was the caretaker. I remember following him around—little snapshots of Amos fixing the toilet or repairing the driveway."

"He's still the caretaker—or was until he broke his foot."

Joelle stared. "He's been here all these years? Why in the world did he stay?"

Tyler's expression softened. "He said he was waiting on you girls to return."

"Oh!" She covered her mouth with her hand as her eyes watered with potential tears. "That's so lovely…and sad. I'm glad he was still alive to see us return."

"Me, too."

All the events of the day rushed in, overwhelming her, and Joelle choked back a sob. "Well, I was about to jump in the shower."

Tyler nodded. "Go ahead. I have some things to finish up here, then I'll need one myself."

She hurried upstairs and hopped in, almost weeping with relief as the steamy water ran over her tired, filthy body. Forcing her mind to a blank slate, she felt her muscles start to loosen. No doubt, she could stand here for hours—or until the hot water ran out—but that probably wouldn't be fair to Tyler, who'd earned his hot shower as much as she had. She lathered up her hair and body and rinsed, then dried off, pulled on her robe and headed into her bedroom.

Now, squeaky clean, she had a completely different dilemma—bra or no bra. Normally, after-shower time was her favorite part of the wardrobe day. Everything restrictive came off and comfortable worn clothes went on, but normally, she wasn't bunking with a bodyguard.

A hot bodyguard.

She shook her head, not about to let her mind dwell on the fact that she was locked in a spooky old house, completely cut off from the rest of the world, and her protector was the most attractive man she'd ever seen up close and personal. Fortunately, his personality dimmed any carnal thoughts she might have had if the circumstances had been different, and that was a really good thing. The last thing Joelle needed was a random fling with a man who clearly had issues with intimacy.

Sighing, she pulled a sports bra out of her suitcase. It was a reasonable compromise and would allow her to venture downstairs to fix something to eat without feeling cheap and loose. Given her luck lately, she might need to sleep in it. A mental visual of fleeing the house in the rainstorm and being collected by Carter or his deputy came to the forefront of her mind. Probably because she'd seen it played out over and over in late-night suspense movies.

Of course, in the movies, the sexy hero always rescued the beautiful heroine and then gave her a passionate kiss, which led to them living happily ever after with a cottage and a golden retriever. She sighed again. And that's exactly why movies were fiction. She dug into her suitcase again and pulled out a book. Sleep wasn't easy for her under the best of circumstances and she'd packed several books, figuring on long, sleepless nights.

She glanced down at the title, then pulled the rest of the books out and scattered them on the bed. Romances. Every single book. She was batting a thousand. Where was a nice boring literary work when you needed it? She scooped all but one of the books up and tossed them back in the suitcase before zipping it and placing it in the corner next to the bed.

The remaining book, she placed on the nightstand next to the lantern. The beds all contained rumpled covers from the night before. After their dash downstairs, no one had felt like going back to bed, so they'd sat in the kitchen, drinking coffee and trying to ready themselves for the exhumation. Joelle pulled the sheets and blankets straight on all three beds and placed the pillows neatly against the headboards, wishing her sisters were joining her again tonight.

It was such a big room for one person.

Last night, with all three of them in there, it had seemed so much smaller, so cozy and intimate, but tonight it almost felt institutional, not dissimilar to the orphanages she frequented. She thought briefly about moving to one of the smaller rooms, but except for the one Tyler occupied, none of the others had been cleaned. The last thing she felt like doing this late was tackling cleaning one of those cluttered, filthy rooms, especially given that she'd already showered.

First thing tomorrow, she'd find a better location and get it ready for occupancy. A single bedroom wouldn't feel as lonely. But now, it was time to rustle up dinner.

As she walked down the hall, the door to the bathroom swung open and Tyler walked out, a wave of steam following him. He wore only sweatpants, and his ripped chest and abdomen still glistened with moisture. She was struck momentarily silent as she took in every single perfect inch of him.

When she realized she was assessing him like a twenty-ounce porterhouse steak, she yanked her gaze up to his face and saw a hint of a smile lurking behind his otherwise blank expression. A blush ran up her neck because she'd been caught ogling him.

"I was, uh," she stammered, "I was headed downstairs to fix something to eat. There're leftover finger sandwiches, crackers and stuff from last night. I know Alaina stocked the refrigerator with meat and stuff, but I was afraid to start cooking lest the power go out in the middle."

You're rambling.

She clamped her mouth shut as his smile broadened. Damn him! He was actually enjoying her discomfort. That was *so* not the behavior of a movie hero.

"Leftovers are fine," he said finally. "Let me grab a shirt and some shoes and I'll join you."

She watched him as he walked away. His backside was just as impressive as the front. As he started to walk into his bedroom, he glanced back and grinned. She whipped around, holding in a groan, and ran straight into the kitchen, where she opened the refrigerator door and promptly stuck her head inside.

What in the world has gotten into me?

She hadn't behaved that way since she was an awkward teen—far, far in the past. Now she was a successful, educated woman who'd had at least one serious relationship and several semi-serious ones. Yet, here she was, almost thirty years old and acting like she was fifteen and he was a star from *Twilight*.

The night just kept getting longer.

THE LIGHT SHINING in her eyes awakened Joelle, and she put one hand up to shield herself as she leaned up in bed. Her book lay beside her, long since forgotten when she nodded off reading it. Assuming she left the lamp on, she turned to the side, and froze when she saw that the lamp didn't emit even a hint of a glow. She bolted upright, trying to ascertain where the light came from, and finally found the source in the far corner of the bedroom.

And that's when panic set in.

The light shimmering in the corner was tall— at least five feet from the floor to the top of it— and as it grew brighter, it began to take shape. Joelle fixed her gaze on it, afraid to even blink, and gasped as the lines of light grew solid and formed the outline of a human body.

I'm dreaming.

It wasn't a bad idea, except for the part where she was positive she was awake.

I'm imagining it.

Also not a bad idea, except for the part where she had twenty-twenty vision and was completely sane.

She reached for her pistol, resting on the edge of the nightstand, and gripped the cold metal in her hands. It seemed silly given that the corporeal being was anything but human, but the weight of the gun made her feel better.

The light seemed to pulse, and then the figure in the center sharpened once more and Joelle gasped.

Mother!

There was no mistaking those high cheekbones, the wide-set eyes and the big smile. Her long hair seemed to billow around her, as if caught in a breeze. Her long white gown rippled along with her hair as she drew closer to the bed.

"You came," her mother said. "I was afraid you wouldn't find your way back here. I waited for you."

A sob broke through and Joelle dropped her hands, letting the gun fall out of her grasp and onto the bed. "I'm so sorry. I didn't know."

"I waited for you, but I grow weak."

The light started to drift back from the bed and Joelle sprang up and hurried to the end of the bed. "Wait! Please don't go. We're trying to find you. Do you know where you are?"

The ghost looked confused for a moment, then gave her a sad look. "I'm here. And then I'm not. I grow weak, but I waited. Now, you need to go."

"Go where?"

"Away from here. It's not safe. I'm tired."

The light began to fade and Joelle reached out one hand. "Please don't leave me."

"I'm here. Sometimes. And then I'm not. I'm here…"

And with one last flicker, the light disappeared completely, casting the room into complete darkness.

Joelle jumped out of bed and ran to the corner, waving her hands around. The hair on her arms stood on end from the electrical charge, but otherwise, no indication remained that something had been here before.

She went back to the bed and flopped down on the end of it. No one would believe her. With all the stress she was under, everyone would assume she dreamed it, or imagined it, or drank heavily. Heck, if she was someone else and heard this story, she'd think the same thing.

Now that the light was gone, the room was so dark, she couldn't even see her hand in front of her face. She'd fallen asleep with the lamp on, so she assumed the power had gone out sometime during the night. She glanced at her watch and saw it was 3:00 a.m. Way too early to be awake, but she seriously doubted she'd be able to go back to sleep. Maybe she'd suggest to Tyler that they purchase a generator and spotlights and do all the work at night and sleep during the day.

Yeah, he wouldn't think that was strange at all.

She crawled across the bed and picked up the lantern, but couldn't even see well enough to light it. Thankful she'd brought the lantern and a flashlight, she picked up the flashlight and clicked it on. The beam of light cast directly at the paned-glass patio doors that led onto the balcony off the bedroom.

At first, the light reflected across the glass, causing a glare. Then her vision sharpened and she saw a masked face staring through the door at her.

Chapter Ten

A bloodcurdling scream sent Tyler vaulting straight up out of bed, grabbing his pistol on the way. He bolted down the hall to Joelle's room and tried to open the door, but it was still locked from the inside. Cursing himself for telling her to draw the inside dead bolt, he banged on the door, yelling for her to open it and hoping like hell she was in a position to do so.

He was just about to start kicking it open when he heard the dead bolt slide back. Joelle threw open the door and pointed to the balcony.

"He was there," she said, her voice breaking, "looking through the door."

Tyler rushed across the room and threw open the patio door, Joelle close behind. He took her flashlight and leaned over the railing, shining it on the kitchen patio. The stone patio wouldn't leave any indication that someone had passed, but he could see branches broken at the edge of the patio where the swamp began. Maybe the damage was from the storm, but it was possible it was from something else.

"Come with me," he said and ran down the hallway.

He looked back as he skipped down the stairs two at a time, figuring he might need to slow down so that Joelle could keep up, but either fear or excellent conditioning had her keeping pace. Satisfied that she was still in sight, he took off at a dead run as soon as he hit the entry floor and rushed out onto the kitchen patio.

Shining the flashlight into the brush at the edge of the patio, he saw the signs that something big had passed through here and without regard to covering its passage. He directed the light to the ground and saw the clear print of a hiking boot where the rain had washed the leaves away, leaving a patch of mud.

If Joelle wasn't there, he'd take off into the swamp after him, but he couldn't leave her unprotected. Purcell's death had already unearthed several people with hidden agendas at the estate. He had no reason to assume only one man was left to carry on business now, or that multiple people were acting independently of each other. Carter had already said that since the start of the events, he'd always felt that whatever was going on was more organized than it seemed.

Luring Tyler away from the house might be just what they wanted to do.

"Let's get back inside," Tyler said.

He waited until Joelle hurried into the kitchen, then pulled the patio door shut, sliding the dead bolt back into place. Even under the cover of the balcony, the steady flow of rain had blown across them, leaving them both damp.

A stack of folded towels and rags sat at the end of the breakfast table and Joelle pulled two off the top and handed one to him. "I never got around to putting them up last night," she said as she ran the towel across her face.

"You're not the housekeeper. I don't expect you to clean up after everyone," he said as he lit the lantern on the kitchen cabinets. The light started small, then grew into a large flame, casting a dim yellow glow across the kitchen.

She shrugged. "Someone's got to do it, and sometimes doing mundane things helps my focus."

Tyler wiped his face and arms and nodded. He understood exactly what she meant. He'd spent countless hours volunteering for hard labor because he needed to work out a security problem that he hadn't found a good solution for. Manual labor unlocked his creativity in a way sitting and pondering never did.

He looked over at Joelle as she wiped her arms with the towel and his eyes locked on her thin white

T-shirt, currently clinging to her otherwise bare breasts. Before she looked up, he managed to avert his eyes, but no way was he going to be able to get that image out of his head.

Joelle was quite simply the most beautiful woman he'd ever encountered.

He held in a sigh that his mind had finally admitted what his body had known from the first moment he'd met her. Why couldn't she have been the ugly sister? Wasn't every family supposed to have one? Instead, all three of Ophelia LeBeau's daughters looked as if they'd stepped off the pages of magazines, and with seemingly no effort if the amount of time they spent getting ready the prior morning was any indication.

Life simply wasn't fair.

Growing up in Calais, he'd dated pretty girls, nice girls and girls with great personalities, but in the years he'd been away, all of the ones who were "wife material" had settled down with Calais boys or moved away to capture bigger fish. He'd expected his return to Calais to be "safe" in far more ways than just physically, especially since according to reports from William, the only single women in Calais were newly widowed grandmothers.

His dad had conveniently forgotten the LeBeau sisters in his statement. Or maybe it had been a deliberate oversight.

Tyler knew his father wanted to see him paired

up and happy, as he and Tyler's mom had been for so many years before she passed away. But that sort of life wasn't on Tyler's radar. Not now. Not ever. Which was why staring at beautiful women's essentially naked breasts was something he had absolutely no business indulging in.

"What happened, exactly?" he asked, trying to get his focus back on track.

"I woke up…and the room was dark. I'd fallen asleep with the lamp on, so I figured the power was out. I turned on the flashlight so that I could see to light the lantern and that's when I saw him."

"Did you recognize him?"

She shook her head. "He was wearing a black mask. When I screamed, he vaulted over the railing."

"Was he trying to get in the room?"

Her eyes widened. "I don't know. I guess that makes sense, right?"

"But you didn't hear anything?"

"No. I think that's why it was such a shock when I saw him. Is it important that I didn't hear anything?"

He shrugged. "I'm just trying to figure out what woke you up at three a.m. and bothered you enough that you wanted to turn on the lantern."

"I…I don't know. I'd fallen asleep with the lamp on, but when I woke up, it was so dark…" She rubbed the towel across her already dry face and looked down at the floor.

"Yeah, that's what you said." Tyler would bet anything he had that she was lying. But why? What did she have to gain from keeping things from him when his only objective was to protect her?

"Are you sure that's all?" Tyler asked. "Because you don't strike me as the kind of woman who is afraid of the dark."

She looked back up at him and he could see the hesitation in her eyes.

"I can't do my job effectively," he said, "if I don't have all the facts."

She shook her head. "You'll think I'm crazy."

"Trust me, after everything my dad's told me, I will not think you're crazy. There's an explanation for everything happening in this house. We just have to find it."

He hadn't convinced her completely, which made him even more curious as to what she was hiding. She pulled at the bottom of her T-shirt for a couple of seconds, then finally sighed.

"I'll tell you, but can we make some coffee and change clothes first? I'm not going to be able to go back to sleep and I want to make sure my head is straight before I try to explain it to you."

"Sure," he said. "You go ahead and change. I'll put the coffee on."

He watched her as she trailed out of the kitchen,

wondering if whatever had awakened her tonight was the same thing that had scared her in the hallway the night before. Either way, he planned on pushing that issue, as well.

Now was not the time for secrets.

JOELLE SNAGGED A dry shirt and a sports bra and hurried back to the bathroom. She'd pulled her long hair back in a ponytail before she'd headed to bed, but she released it now so that the thin sheen of rain that covered it would dry more quickly. As she reached for the hem of her T-shirt, she glanced in the mirror and groaned. The thin white cotton was just damp enough to be completely sheer. She may as well have been standing shirtless in the kitchen.

This is what you get for taking off the sports bra.

She tugged off the damp garment and wiped her body with the towel to remove any remaining moisture. It wasn't enough that she had to go downstairs and tell Tyler she'd seen a ghost—who'd talked to her, no less. But she had to do so with the knowledge that he'd seen half of her practically naked.

Pulling her bra and dry shirt over her head, she marveled at his self-control. He'd never given any indication that she was essentially half-clad. Not a single flicker, wide eye or half smile. He either had the self-control of an android or he wasn't interested in what he'd seen.

She took another critical look at herself. Considering she was being stalked and haunted and had just learned her mother's body was missing from her grave, she thought she looked pretty good. Her body was a combination of Alaina and Danae. She'd gotten Alaina's height and Danae's curves. It was a good combination and one she knew attracted male attention. And although she didn't have her mother's fine bone structure like Alaina, her face was nice. Her hair—thanks to a genius hairstylist—was stellar.

Definitely android.

And completely unfair. She'd practically drooled at his bare chest the night before and he hadn't returned the favor. Okay, rude *and* unfair.

She ran her fingers through her hair to fluff it out some, then tossed the towel over the shower rod and headed downstairs, unable to think of a good reason to delay the conversation she had no desire to have.

Tyler hadn't changed clothes, but then his T-shirt was black, not see-through, and even if it had been, those rules didn't apply to men. He poured two cups of coffee when he saw her enter the kitchen.

"How do you take it?"

"Normally with lots of sugar and cream, but I think I'll go with black."

"Black it is," he said and carried the mugs to the breakfast table.

She dropped into a chair and took a sip of the

hot, steamy liquid. The bitter taste gave her a momentary shock, but she figured it would also keep her sharp. Her story wasn't going to go over well with Tyler. He was a no-nonsense sort of guy, and what she was about to say was definitely nonsense. At least, that's what she'd think if she hadn't seen it herself.

"So," he said. "You were going to tell me what woke you up?"

"I'll tell you, but you're not going to like it."

"I didn't figure I would, but that doesn't eliminate the need for hearing it."

"Fine." She took a deep breath and then proceeded to explain her awakening to the light—how it changed form to become her mother—how it spoke to her.

She had to give him credit. He listened intently, never interrupting and without so much as a raised eyebrow. If roles had been reversed, she'd have been looking for a psych referral form a long time ago.

"And then the light just faded away," she finished.

Tyler stared at her for a long time, slightly frowning.

"I told you that you'd think I was crazy," she said, unable to keep the frustration out of her voice.

"I don't think you're crazy," he said quietly.

"No, you probably think I dreamed it or imagined it due to stress or something."

"I think you saw exactly what you say you saw."

Her jaw dropped a bit and she stared at him, looking for any indication that he was humoring her, but his expression was completely serious.

"I just want to be clear. You believe the ghost of my mother came to visit me and spoke?"

He nodded. "You seem surprised."

"Surprised is the understatement of the decade. I'm completely blown away. Do you know what I would tell anyone who tried to pass off a story like that to me?"

He smiled. "That they were crazy?"

"For starters. Should I even ask why this doesn't freak you out?"

He shrugged. "I've seen a lot of things I couldn't explain. There's a lot of myth and legend buried in Mystere Parish swamps. Some people believe the swamp itself is a living, breathing entity and that it sometimes comes alive if things are out of balance."

"People believe in a swamp god?"

"No, people believe the swamp is a force of nature that will act to change things it doesn't like."

"Who believes this?"

"My dad, for starters. Me, Carter, Carter's mom…truth be known, probably everyone who's lived near the swamp their whole lives believes it, even though some wouldn't admit it."

Joelle leaned back in her chair and stared at him. "I can't believe it. Here I am all worried about what you think, and you're telling me straight out that I saw a ghost."

"You're not the first to see her."

She sat straight up again, jostling her coffee. "What?"

"Alaina and Danae have both seen her, and Danae's fiancé, Zach."

She sucked in a breath, her mind racing with this new bit of information. "Why didn't they tell me last night?"

"Maybe because you would have thought they were crazy? I'm just guessing that it's not the kind of conversation sisters want to lead off with after a twenty-five-year separation. I'm sure they were planning on telling you soon—might have today— but the exhumation kind of put a kink in things."

"Hmm." She couldn't come up with any viable comment.

"Did you see her that first night?" he asked. "Right before you heard the intruder?"

"No," she said quickly.

"Then what did you see, and don't tell me nothing. You had that same look then as you did when you let me in your bedroom tonight. Something spooked you."

She clenched her hands and stared down at them, not wanting to share such a horrible memory. Not wanting to repeat it out loud. "I remembered some-

thing from my childhood. No ghosts—just the recollection of a child."

"Why did it scare you?"

"I was standing on the balcony. I was supposed
to be asleep, but I was peeking through the banisters and looking downstairs at my mom and Purcell. They were arguing. He…he was an evil man.
I felt it long before I knew any of the things he did."

She looked up at him. "I don't like remembering my stepfather. It's almost like he's right there
with me all over again. He always scared me."

She watched him closely. His expression softened
and she relaxed a bit. He'd bought her story. Not
that it wasn't true—Purcell had always frightened
her—but she hadn't told him everything. Hadn't
told him that she was sure Purcell had physically
abused her mother their entire relationship. How
could she share such a personal thing that didn't
matter to anyone any longer, except her? Joelle
knew how normal people viewed abused women.
Most blamed the victim for the abuse, not bothering
to try to understand the dynamics in play. William
said everyone in Calais had loved Ophelia. Joelle
wasn't about to do anything to change that.

Tyler sighed. "I would say he can't hurt you now,
but that's not exactly true. I wish I could say something that made it better. I guess the only thing I've
got is that you can be certain Purcell didn't win.
He didn't get the money. He had to remain hidden

in this house for the last third of his miserable life, hustling family heirlooms to pay people for silence. I guarantee you, that's not what he planned."

Joelle gave him a small smile. "That does make me feel a tiny bit better. Do you think that's why my mother's ghost haunts the house—because Purcell killed her?"

"It would be as good a reason as any."

"You said Alaina and Danae saw her. Did she talk to them, too?"

"I heard it all thirdhand through my dad, but according to him, she didn't speak to Alaina but she did to Danae."

"What did she say?"

"She kept repeating 'so close.'"

Joelle frowned. "So close? What does that mean?"

Tyler shook his head. "No one knows. It could be a lot of things."

"Or it could be nothing."

"What do you mean?"

Joelle took a minute to think of a good way to explain what she'd felt during her interaction. "She seemed confused…like she wasn't sure how she got here, and she also said she's weak. Maybe she's not strong enough to appear and manage coherent thought."

He blew out a breath. "I suppose anything's possible. If it requires a lot of effort for her to appear, she may be using all her energy and focus just on that."

Another thought flashed through Joelle's mind and she crossed her arms and shivered. "Or maybe she's lost in limbo somewhere...because her body is lost."

Tyler placed his hand on her arm. "She's not lost. She's just not readily visible. We're going to figure all this out."

"I know you believe that, and I want to, but it all happened so long ago. What if it's not possible to unravel it all?"

She reached for her cup of coffee, eager to feel the warm cup between her hands. Tyler never answered her, and that pretty much said it all.

Chapter Eleven

It was barely 7:00 a.m. when Tyler dropped Joelle off at Carter's house to talk with Alaina. He waved from the truck and headed into town, hoping to catch Carter having breakfast at the café. The list of things they needed to discuss was growing by the second, and the steady drizzle was preventing any contact by phone.

Carter was perched on his usual stool at the counter, and looked a bit surprised when Tyler slid onto the seat beside him.

"Morning, Tyler." The waitress, Sonia, smiled at him as she slid a cup of coffee in front of him. "Saw you on the sidewalk and figured you'd be wanting a cup. You hungry?"

Tyler looked over at Carter. "You eating?"

"Am I breathing?"

Tyler grinned and turned back to Sonia. "I'll take the special."

Sonia made a note on her pad and stuck the ticket

up next to the grill, then hurried into the café to refill coffee cups.

Johnny, the café owner, turned from the grill and winked at Tyler. "Looks like you lost your boyish charm."

Tyler laughed. "Apparently so."

"What do you mean?" Carter asked.

Johnny grinned. "Sonia used to chase after him so hard he stopped coming in here with his daddy for a good month. Heck, I figure he went into the marines as much to get away from Sonia as to have a job."

Carter smiled. "She was dating a guy in New Orleans—even moved there for a while—but apparently it didn't work out and she landed back in Calais a month ago."

"Yep," Johnny said. "One of them numbers guys—finance, stock…something like that. Never sounded like a good fit to me. Sonia's a great gal, but she's more of a *Field & Stream* type than *Wall Street Journal,* if you know what I mean."

Tyler nodded at Johnny's accurate description.

"Worked out fine for me, though," Johnny continued, "as Danae gave her notice and claimed her fortune. Anyway, I got some stock to get in the refrigerator before it spoils, then I'll start your breakfast."

Johnny paused for a moment, then looked a bit

embarrassed. "I don't usually say things like this, but it's good to see you two sitting here again."

"It's good being here again," Tyler said.

"Absolutely," Carter agreed.

Johnny gave them a nod and headed through a door to the back room of the café.

"You're up and out early," Carter said, as soon as Johnny was out of hearing distance.

"Been up for hours. The out part is recent."

Carter's eyebrows went up. "Any particular reason you've been up for hours?"

"More than one, and that's part of the reason I'm here." Tyler gave Carter a recount of the night's events, only leaving out the part about Joelle's sheer breast display. It had certainly made an impact on Tyler's night, but it wasn't relevant to the investigation.

Carter's scowl told Tyler everything the good sheriff thought about the situation. "You check for tracks off the patio?"

"Yep, but I lost them ten yards in when the ground cover got too thick to leave prints. The storm caused too much damage to the foliage to tell the difference after a while. It was easy to see where he barreled into the swamp, but my guess is that he slowed up when no one pursued him and got more deliberate about his path choice."

"I'm sure you're right. So what do you make of this ghost thing?"

Tyler shook his head. "I was going to ask you that question. You know more about it than I do, and heard some of it firsthand."

"You're sure Joelle saw her mother's ghost?"

"I don't think she imagined it. She was wide awake when she let me in the room, and something got her out of bed or she wouldn't have seen the intruder to begin with."

"And the ghost told her to leave the house?"

"Yeah. Said it wasn't safe."

Carter blew out a breath. "Which we already know, but why now? It wasn't safe before but she didn't try to warn off Alaina or Danae."

Tyler remembered Joelle's thoughts on the ghost. "Joelle wonders if the spirit is completely aware—like maybe the energy it takes her to appear leaves her confused on other things."

"If that's the case, it's damned inconvenient."

"No kidding."

"Any ideas on what to do about it?"

"The ghost? Heck no. The Marine Corps didn't offer training for that problem. On the security end of things, I got the inside cameras hooked up. With no internet, it's not as easy to cover a lot of area. Hiding the wiring presents some challenges. I think we're fine as long as he enters at night, but if he comes in during the day and looks closely, he may pick up on the cameras."

"Any progress on entry?"

"None, and it's really bugging me. The house is locked up tight. Every window is nailed shut. The dead bolts are pulled on the patio and laundry room doors, and the front door is equipped with an alarm."

"But yet, he still got in night before last."

"The front door didn't have an alarm then," Tyler pointed out.

"Yeah, I know, but the front door angle is too simple." Carter blew out a breath of frustration. "I've had this feeling all along that I'm missing something. That it's right under my nose and I haven't seen it yet. Do you know what I mean?"

Tyler nodded. He knew exactly what Carter meant because he felt it, too. Like every second he spent in that house was a second where he was at a disadvantage.

"I'll keep looking," Tyler said. "He can't hide forever."

"I'm glad you're there, man. I hate to admit it, but I'm running out of ideas. A fresh look by someone with a different perspective might open an avenue I hadn't considered."

Tyler nodded, pleased with Carter's faith in him. When they were in high school—Tyler the quiet freshman and Carter the football-star senior—he'd always admired Carter and wished he could be more like him. He'd managed to develop a more outgoing personality and his own level of high school success before graduating and leaving for the Marine Corps, but his high opinion of Carter Trahan had held fast.

"So how are other things?" Carter asked.

"What other things?"

Carter grinned. "C'mon, I've seen Joelle. You're a red-blooded American man, spending every waking hour with her at arm's length. Don't tell me you haven't noticed she's a looker."

The last thing Tyler was going to admit to Carter was that he'd noticed entirely too much about the way Joelle looked. "Aren't you marrying her sister?" he asked.

Carter laughed. "That doesn't mean I'm blind or dead, or that I'm too dazed to know a deflection when I hear it."

"No deflection. I'm just there to do my job."

"I see. It's all a professional thing."

"Exactly."

"Uh-huh. It was a professional thing when I agreed to verify the heirs' presence for the estate, and I ended up engaged to the first one I met."

Tyler studied Carter for a moment. He was the last guy Tyler had ever imagined would be cozied up with a fiancée. According to William, they were about to break ground on a bigger house and possibly acquire a golden retriever. It was so incredibly domestic for the man he'd once thought was a superhero. But the strangest part of it all was how happy he looked about the entire thing.

"You're really happy," Tyler said.

Carter smiled. "Seems strange, right? If anyone had told me a year ago that I'd be back in Calais and living with a woman I planned to marry, I'd have called them crazy. But yeah, I'm happier than I've ever been."

"It doesn't seem strange—this pace after working for the New Orleans Police Department?"

"Not lately," Carter joked, "but all Purcell business aside, it felt slow and dull for several months. Then I started developing a rhythm. I think my body and mind needed time to decompress."

Tyler considered Carter's words. Maybe his friend was right. Maybe he just needed some time to adjust, and then everything would feel right.

"You feeling restless?" Carter asked.

Tyler nodded, not the least bit surprised that Carter had picked up on his state of flux. Everyone swore that Carter's mother, Willamina, was darn near psychic, and most thought Carter had inherited his mother's ability to read people.

"I don't know why, though," Tyler said. "I couldn't wait to leave Calais when I graduated high school. I did a good job for the Marine Corps—more than my share of overseas tours—and I have no regrets about leaving the military."

"But?"

"It's hard to explain."

Carter took a sip of his coffee. "You feel like you can't get firm ground beneath you. Like no matter where you go or what you do, you don't fit."

Tyler stared. "Yeah. That's it exactly."

Carter nodded. "I felt that way when I came back. My mom says it's because humans are always looking for a constant, and life doesn't have any. She thinks that when we accept that everything changes and that the only thing we have control over is ourselves, that the feeling of restlessness goes away."

Tyler mulled that theory over for a minute. Finally, he shook his head. "Your mother is a genius."

Carter laughed and clapped Tyler's back. "Don't tell her that. She doesn't need any more people in this town telling her how great she is."

Tyler smiled, a tiny inkling of what his life could be starting to creep through his closed mind. "Sorry, but I've always thought she was the bomb. I'm unable to hide it. Hey, did you ever wonder why our parents haven't hooked up?"

Carter's expression changed from laughter to slightly mortified. "No, I never wondered that. I don't ever put 'hooked up' and thoughts of my mom in the same realm."

"That's because she's your mother and a lady, but if William were your dad, what would you think?"

Carter's brow scrunched for several seconds,

then he sighed. "I guess I'd be wondering why he wasn't chasing my mother. But can we leave that up to them? I love your dad, but I don't want the visual."

Tyler smiled at Carter's obvious discomfort, but the question was one he'd wondered about for quite some time. Both his dad and Willamina had been widowed for a long time, and neither had established another relationship that he was aware of. They'd known each other since they were kids, seemed to enjoy each other's company and planned to stay in Calais the rest of their lives. It was the perfect fit.

"Maybe I'll ask my dad about it sometime," Tyler said.

"Ha. Do that and you'll be inviting your dad to point out that you're currently living with a drop-dead gorgeous heiress. He spent some time trying to convince me that I needed to settle down. Pointed out every single woman under fifty, like I didn't already know them all."

"You're kidding? Wow, I guess I'll leave that door shut, then."

"He'll get around to it anyway. He's just waiting for an opportunity."

"He can get around to it all he wants, but it's not going to happen."

Carter took another sip of his coffee. "So you said."

JOELLE CLIMBED OUT of Alaina's car in front of the prettiest house she'd ever seen, not even the constant drizzle able to diminish its loveliness. It was Southern, with white siding and bright white columns across the front. The landscaping looked like something from the White House grounds and nothing she'd expected to see in the middle of the swamp.

"Isn't it beautiful?" Alaina said as they walked to the front door. "Willamina should have been a professional landscaper."

"She did all this herself?"

Alaina nodded. "She hires local teens for some of the manual labor, but the design is all hers."

"It's amazing."

Alaina grinned. "Wait until you see the back."

"Are you sure this is okay? It's really early to visit someone, especially when she didn't even know we were coming until ten minutes ago."

"If Willamina found out you were at my house and I didn't bring you to meet her, she'd never let me live it down. Besides, I'm fairly certain she's a vampire. I've never once caught her sleeping."

Alaina rang the doorbell and a couple seconds later, an attractive, silver-haired woman opened the door and waved them in. She gave Alaina a hug, then turned to Joelle with a big smile.

"You look like your father," Willamina said. "He was a handsome man, but I think his features look even better on a woman. You're absolutely gorgeous."

Joelle flushed at the compliment, not used to people being so direct.

Willamina smiled. "And I've embarrassed you. How delightful!" She threw her arms around Joelle and squeezed her.

Joelle hugged her back, surprised that her discomfort level was quickly subsiding.

"It's a pleasure to meet you," Joelle said when Willamina released her. "Alaina has told me so many good things about you."

Willamina beamed at Alaina, and Joelle could tell how much Willamina adored her future daughter-in-law. "Alaina is a real treasure. I couldn't have picked a better woman for Carter if I'd done it myself, and don't think I didn't consider it."

Joelle smiled at the thought of Willamina pushing a woman on Carter. That would be a battle worthy of box seats.

"I have quiche and blueberry tarts ready in the kitchen, and I've set up the patio for breakfast. We're having mimosas and I don't want to hear a single complaint about calories."

"Woo-hoo!" Alaina said as she headed off to what Joelle assumed was the kitchen. "You'll never hear me complaining about champagne for breakfast. Wait until you taste her tarts, Joelle."

"We better hurry," Willamina said, "or she'll

drink all the good stuff." She linked her arm through Joelle's and guided her through the house to the huge kitchen off the back. It had miles of granite countertops and top-of-the-line appliances. Huge windows and patio doors allowed light to stream inside, making the entire room bright despite the fact that the overhead lights weren't even turned on.

"This is beautiful," Joelle said. "Your entire home is beautiful and the landscaping is the best I've ever seen."

Willamina beamed. "Thank you so much, dear. Cooking and planting are my two biggest loves."

Alaina picked up a tray of tarts to carry outside. "It's a good thing she loves manual labor, because with her cooking, a sedentary lifestyle would be killer. I've had to add an extra two miles to my daily run just to keep the pounds off."

Joelle picked up the champagne glasses and followed Alaina out on a huge covered patio. It overlooked the well-manicured backyard that covered a couple of acres before ending at a line of cypress trees that formed the edge of the swamp. She could hear running water nearby and figured a bayou ran just past the line of cypress trees.

It was as lovely as the woman who cared for it, and Joelle understood why Alaina had insisted she meet Willamina.

"So," Willamina said after they'd taken their

seats and dug into the truly incredible quiche. "Alaina tells me that Tyler Duhon is your personal bodyguard."

"Yes, ma'am."

"Please, call me Willa. I'm not old enough to be ma'am yet. I've known Tyler since he was born. He was a beautiful baby, and seems to me that hasn't changed."

Joelle laughed. "Are you calling Tyler beautiful?"

Willamina smiled. "Heavens, no. You can't say that about grown men, even if it's true. What I would say is that he's a fine specimen and just as handsome as his father was back in the day. Tyler's got a much better body than his father ever did, though. I suppose the military did that."

Alaina snorted and grabbed her napkin. "I totally got champagne up my nose. Willa, you're awful!"

"I suppose he is quite attractive," Joelle acquiesced.

Willamina shook her head. "Don't play dumb with me. I know you've got better eyesight than that. Please tell me you've gotten a glimpse of him in some state of undress."

Joelle felt a blush creep up her neck and Willamina hooted.

"I knew it," Willamina said. "Tell all."

Joelle was completely mortified, but knew she had to say something or Willamina would never let her off the hook. "I saw him when he came out of the shower last night. I hate to disappoint you, but he was wearing sweats."

"Ah, but he wasn't wearing a shirt." Willamina nodded at Alaina, who just smiled at her future mother-in-law. "So is he a finely tuned machine under that cotton?"

"He definitely works out."

Willamina rolled her eyes. "I can see that with the clothes on. Give an old widow a thrill."

Joelle sighed. "He's absolutely perfect. In fact, I've never seen anyone with such a perfect body except in magazines."

"And they're airbrushed," Alaina pointed out. "So that makes Tyler even better."

Willamina nodded, then patted Joelle's arm. "See, that wasn't so hard."

Willamina's obvious delight was so clear that Joelle couldn't help adopting the lighthearted mood. These were good women—one of them her sister. If she couldn't speak honestly with them, she couldn't with anyone.

"I didn't want people to get the wrong idea," Joelle said, trying to explain her hesitation.

"Honey," Willamina said, "I've got all kinds of ideas for the two of you, and none of them are wrong."

"No!" Joelle stared. "I have no intention—"

"Neither did I," Alaina said and smiled. "And you see how that turned out."

The last vestige of holding out fled from her and Joelle laughed. "You win. I took one look at his bare chest and my mind went places it had no business going. His backside is just as perfect, by the way. But even if I was interested in a relationship, I get the idea that it's the last thing Tyler wants."

"Why is that?" Alaina asked.

"He's distant. Don't get me wrong, he can be very nice and surprisingly intuitive, but the instant I try to turn the conversation to anything personal, he clams up and bolts."

The smile faded from Willamina's face and she nodded. "William is worried about him. I have to agree that he's not the same man who left here eight years ago, but how could he be? We can only imagine the atrocities he faced overseas. He needs some time to shed the worst of them, but that doesn't mean he's not still a red-blooded man."

Joelle's mind flashed back to several hours before, when she'd stood in the kitchen, her damp T-shirt leaving nothing to the imagination. "I don't know about the red-blooded part," she said, then told them about her grossly embarrassing T-shirt mishap.

Willamina waved a hand in dismissal. "That's just manners. If he had stared, his mother would have popped straight up out of her grave and given him the what for."

"Maybe," Joelle said, but she couldn't shake the

feeling that his failure to respond like the average male was due more to disinterest than manners.

"You aren't serious with anyone, right?" Alaina asked. "I mean, the other night, you said you were single, but you seemed to hesitate when you said that."

"I'm single," Joelle assured her. "I guess I'm still a bit aggravated because that's the case."

"Was there someone before you came here?" Alaina asked.

"Yes. Brad. We met in college and dated for over five years. I thought we were on our way to white picket fence territory, but apparently that hinged on whether or not I'd change jobs."

"What difference does that make?" Willamina asked.

"Brad never understood why I took a master's degree in psychology and chose to become a social worker. He pictured me with a private practice, maybe even a home office, and couldn't understand why I'd put myself at risk to help battered women and children. When I started volunteering with the underground railroad, it was the final straw for him."

"Good riddance, then," Willamina said. "You're providing an incredible service for people in awful situations. How can that be a bad thing?"

"Intrinsically, it's not. But Brad worried about my safety, as well as his own or that of our kids, in the future. He's not wrong, really. There's always the element of risk that an abuser will take things to a personal level. Look at Brant."

Alaina sighed. "No, he's not wrong. I've seen enough horror in the legal system to know that the danger is very real. But people live with it all the time. Every law enforcement officer, every member of the legal system—"

"Every politician," Willamina interjected.

"Got that right," Alaina agreed. "They're all at risk and yet most of them marry and have families and live without anything untoward happening."

"I know," Joelle said, "but it was still his choice to make, as it was mine to choose to remain doing a job that gives me purpose."

"I still say he was a fool," Willamina said. "That's my choice to make."

Joelle smiled, marveling at how comfortable she felt with Carter's engaging mother. Willamina was everything she wished for the women she helped—strong, independent, intelligent and not the least bit afraid to speak her mind.

"You would be a great influence on the women I work with," Joelle said.

"Me?" Willamina seemed surprised. "Oh, I don't think so."

"She's right," Alaina said. "If Jackson wasn't so far away, you could do group therapy with them.

Just talking to someone with your fortitude might make a difference."

Joelle nodded. "Maybe you won't have to come as far as Jackson."

"What do you mean?" Willamina asked.

"Ever since I talked to William, I've been doing a lot of thinking…about what happens when this is over and the estate is distributed. I think I'd like to open a home for women, where they could live with their children while they learn a job skill and transition into a new life. Give them a safe place to stay and the training they need."

Willamina's eyes misted up. "That's such a wonderful thing to think of."

"What else am I going to do with all that money? I'm not the private-island-and-servant kind of gal."

And it gives me a chance to use my mother's money to help other women in situations similar to hers.

But Joelle wasn't willing to talk about her childhood memories, so she left that part unsaid.

Chapter Twelve

It was almost lunchtime when Tyler pulled through the circular drive in front of the house. Looking up at the depressing structure, Joelle sighed, already missing the company of Alaina and Willamina, who were thoroughly interesting and entertaining.

"We didn't have to leave Calais," Tyler said, apparently cluing in to her less-than-enthusiastic demeanor.

"We have to come back sometime. And it's not as scary during the day. Depressing...but not scary."

They climbed out of the truck and hurried inside before the drizzling rain soaked them. Joelle shrugged off the light jacket she wore and headed to the kitchen, Tyler close behind. She draped her jacket over one of the kitchen chairs, then pulled open the refrigerator and grabbed a bottled water.

"Would you like one?" she asked Tyler, who stood in front of the patio door, staring out into the swamp.

"No, thanks. This rain has ruined any chance of

my tracking the man you saw last night," he said with a sigh. "Any prints he may have left were washed away."

Joelle could practically feel the frustration coming off of him. Tyler was a man of action. Certainly he'd had to exercise patience with his work with the Marine Corps, but the feeling of being trapped here added to the helplessness that Joelle felt about the entire situation. Perhaps Tyler felt the same.

"So what are you planning on doing today?"

He turned around to look at her. "First, I'll check the laptop and make sure we didn't have any activity on the cameras while we were gone."

She froze. "Surely he wouldn't come inside during the day?"

Tyler shrugged. "He could have been watching when we drove off. Or he could have already been inside and heard us leave. Carter thinks that someone was listening to their conversations when Danae was here. The timing of things was too perfect to suspect otherwise."

"He ran away last night," she continued to argue, completely uncomfortable with the idea that he might be in the house with them at this moment. "We would have heard him if he came back in."

Tyler shook his head. "Not if he has another way in—one we don't know about. Carter is convinced there's an alternate entrance to the house, and I'm inclined to agree. I don't think someone's been able to slip unnoticed through the front door all this time."

She frowned. "If he has a way in, then why was he on my balcony last night?"

"I don't know," Tyler said, looking a bit uncomfortable. "Maybe he figured you were locked inside and wanted to assess who was in there with you. He might be willing to risk an attack on one person, but that first night, there were three of you in there."

"Oh." She immediately realized what Tyler was too classy to say—that the intruder was trying to determine if she was sharing a room with Tyler. "So how do we find the entrance?"

"Give me a minute," Tyler said and hurried out of the kitchen. He returned shortly with the laptop he had hidden in one of the front rooms and wired to the motion-activated cameras.

He placed the laptop on the kitchen counter and opened it up. "If he's been inside since I rigged the cameras, I thought they would give us a starting point for finding the entrance."

Joelle moved next to him and watched as he brought up the surveillance software. "Two saved files," she said, her pulse ticking up a bit.

"Nine a.m. for the first video. I hope it's not mice," he said and clicked on the first file.

As soon as the video feed opened, Joelle sucked in a breath. "It's him!"

She leaned forward, trying to make out the grainy infrared video, and saw a dark figure emerge from the kitchen hallway into the entry. He looked upward and then continued ahead until he fell out of sight of the camera.

"Can you zoom in on his face?" she asked.

"Already working on it," Tyler said as he froze the video as the intruder stepped into the entry. He highlighted a section on the video and tapped the mouse pad to expand it.

Tyler cursed as the grainy feed came somewhat into focus. "He's wearing a mask. I figured as much after what you saw last night, but I hoped he'd slip up and remove it when he was inside."

He started the feed again and she pointed at a blur on the screen just before the intruder disappeared behind the camera. "What was that?" she asked. "That blur?"

"Let me see if I can slow it down to get a better look."

He backed up the feed a bit, then inched it forward frame by frame until the intruder was right below the camera. "I still can't make it out. Let me slow it down some more."

He backed the feed up again and moved it forward at an even slower speed. This time, he managed to capture the blur as it was right in front of the camera.

Joelle's eyes widened. "Oh, wow!"

The vulgar hand gesture was grainy, but there was no mistaking it.

Tyler cursed and closed the feed. "He knows the cameras are there."

"But how?"

Tyler shook his head. "Maybe he was inside when I rigged them. Maybe it's because I'm staying here and he was looking for something like this."

"Does everyone know what you did in the service?"

"My dad, Carter, Carter's mom and your sisters for sure. I don't think it's common gossip, but I suppose someone could find out if they tried."

He clicked on the second feed and watched as the intruder walked back down the hall to the kitchen.

"We know he didn't come through the patio door," she said. "So how did he get in? How did he leave? There's no other way out of the house that way except the patio door. Could he have taken the servants' staircase upstairs and left that way?"

Tyler shook his head. "I have a camera pointing at the hallway where that staircase emerges."

"Well, he didn't go into the kitchen and disappear into thin air!"

"No, but he could have walked through the butler's pantry and worked his way around the back side of the house from the formal dining room. The camera doesn't cover that area of the house."

A wave of disappointment washed over her at

their failure to narrow down the possibilities, then suddenly she remembered something. "Come with me," she said and hurried out of the kitchen and around the entry, taking the long way to the formal dining room.

Her pulse quickened as she pointed to the painting of Alaina that she'd unearthed the day before. It was still leaning against the door to the butler's pantry. "I propped it up there yesterday. He couldn't have come through that door without knocking down the painting."

"He could have easily propped it back up afterward."

She sighed. "You're right."

"Let's check again, just to be sure." Tyler walked over to the door and slid the painting to the side. He walked inside the pantry and studied the wall that ran along the exterior of the house. Shaking his head, he pulled open the cabinets and peered inside. "There's no exit here. He can't walk through walls."

She blew out a breath of frustration and slid over to peer inside the cabinets. As she moved, her left foot banged into something small and hard and she stumbled into Tyler. He reached out to steady her, but she caught her balance and took a step back to flip up the end of the rug.

"Holy crap," she said as she stared at the iron ring secured to the wooden floor.

Tyler pulled the rug from the floor and tossed it

in the dining room. The clear outline of a trapdoor stared back at them. He reached for the ring and pulled the trapdoor up, exposing a narrow set of wooden steps that led straight down. Joelle hurried into the kitchen to snag a flashlight, and he shone it down the stairs.

Joelle peered down into the dark hole, thinking it was the last place she wanted to go. "I guess we have to go down there, right?"

Tyler grabbed the lantern from the kitchen and lit it, then handed Joelle the flashlight. "I'll go down first with the lantern. Wait until I tell you to come down. If the steps are rotted…"

He didn't finish but she understood the score. She needed to remain up top in case a call for an ambulance was required. She leaned over, watching as Tyler slowly descended the narrow stairs.

"The stairs are good," he called out when he got to the bottom. "Just be careful. They're narrow."

Joelle tucked the flashlight in her back pocket and, taking a deep breath, stepped down. She clutched the ridges of the trapdoor until she got low enough to grab the railing, then ducked under the edge of the floor. The railing stopped halfway down and Tyler reached up to offer his arm. She held his arm with her right hand, just to keep herself steady, and negotiated the rest of the stairs.

When she got to the bottom, she looked around, somewhat surprised at the size of the room. It was probably twenty feet square with a dirt bottom. At some point, an attempt had been made to finish out the dirt walls, but it wasn't complete. Two walls were covered in paneling, but the other two only contained two-by-four framing.

"I didn't think people had basements in this area. Isn't it below sea level?"

He nodded. "It's not common, that's for sure. But I don't think this is a basement—I mean, not like what you and I know as basements."

She frowned. "It's under the house and surrounded with dirt. What else could it be?"

"A root cellar. The house is over a hundred years old."

Suddenly Joelle understood. "And they didn't have refrigeration then, so they stored perishables underground. That's why the entrance is in the butler's pantry."

Tyler walked slowly around the room, taking in every square inch. When he got back around to Joelle, he shook his head.

"I don't see why anyone would come down here now. It's empty except for that stack of unused lumber."

"Maybe someone used it as a hiding place. I bet you could hear everything said in the kitchen from down here."

"I guess it's possible he could have held the edge of the rug when he pulled the door down. Then no one would have seen it if they passed through here. Still, it's a big risk. There's nowhere to hide if anyone came down here."

"Desperate people do desperate things," she said. "I see it all the time."

Tyler studied her for a moment, then nodded. "I guess you do. Well, there's nothing else to see here, so let's get back upstairs."

Joelle started up the stairs, disappointed that yet another promising lead had turned into nothing. Short of the intruder dropping down a chimney like Santa Claus, she had no clue how he was getting inside the house. She knew Tyler wouldn't stop looking until he found the answer, but what could happen in the meantime? What if someone shot at her through the walls as they had Alaina? What if she couldn't scramble and get away as fast as her marathon-running sister had? Joelle was in good shape, but she definitely wasn't a sprinter.

As she stepped into the kitchen, she felt her cell phone vibrate in her jeans pocket. Hoping it was Alaina or Danae, she pulled it out, then frowned.

"What's wrong?" Tyler asked.

"Unknown number."

"Answer it," he said and stepped close to her. When she put the phone to her ear, he leaned in so that he could hear.

"Hello," she said.

At first, there was only silence, then they could

hear someone breathing. Finally, the phone beeped and she looked at the display.

"The call dropped," she said.

"Or he disconnected. It could have been a wrong number."

Joelle nodded, but something told her it wasn't a wrong number. Something about the breathing had hit a nerve, and somehow she knew it wasn't as simple as a wrong number.

Then the phone vibrated again.

"It's a text," she said and pressed the button to open.

Return what's mine, or maybe I'll take something of yours.

She sucked in a breath so hard it made her dizzy. Tyler put his hands on her shoulders to steady her and looked down at the phone.

"There's something attached to the text," he said.

She blinked twice to clear her vision, then accessed the attachment. As soon as the first picture came into view, she gasped. It was a picture of Danae walking down the sidewalk in front of Zach's condo in New Orleans. She scrolled to the next picture, then the next, her heart pounding harder in her chest with every image—picture after picture of Danae in New Orleans. Then the images shifted to Alaina, and Tyler cursed.

"That's in Calais," he said.

In a daze, Joelle scrolled through the pictures of Alaina entering the general store, getting in her car at Carter's house and walking into the café. When she got to the last image, she dropped the phone.

"No!" she cried.

It was a picture of her, Alaina and Willamina, sitting on Willamina's back patio.

Unable to stand the stress any longer, she burst into tears. Tyler immediately wrapped his arms around her and pulled her to his chest, hugging her tightly. She clutched him, feeling as if she were drowning, and sobbed as she'd never done before.

Tyler stroked her hair and whispered, "It's going to be all right."

Finally, she slumped against him, her body spent. She stayed there for a while, relishing the comfort of his strong arms around her, until she mustered the strength to regain control. Then she looked up at him. "I'm sorry," she said.

"Don't you dare apologize. Anyone in your position would be upset. I'm a half step away from losing it myself."

His expression was a mixture of sympathy, worry and frustration, and Joelle's heart leaped at this man's honor and heart. He may not have wanted this job, but he would risk anything to protect her and her family. In all her life, she'd never met anyone like him, and she doubted she ever would again.

He looked down at her and lifted one hand to wipe a tear from her cheek. "He will not hurt you or your sisters. I won't let that happen."

"I know," she said and believed every word.

He stared at her a moment more and his expression shifted from frustration to something else...something she hadn't seen before. A shiver of excitement ran through her as she realized he was going to kiss her. Before he even lowered his head, her lips were already tingling, waiting for his touch.

When his lips brushed hers, her knees went weak and she had to lock them in place. She slid her arms around him, the feel of his strong back beneath her fingers sending a thrill through her already-stimulated body. He deepened the kiss, and a rush of heat passed over her as she prayed that this was only the beginning.

"Anyone home?" Carter's voice boomed from the entry.

Immediately, Tyler broke off their kiss and released her, then rushed out of the kitchen without so much as a backward glance. Joelle stared after him, not sure whether to be angry that he could switch gears so quickly or angry at Carter for interrupting something that could have gotten very interesting.

What she knew for certain was that a little taste of Tyler Duhon was not nearly enough.

Chapter Thirteen

Tyler strode away from the kitchen wondering what the hell he was thinking. Strike that. He knew exactly what he'd been thinking, but couldn't believe he'd allowed such a slip in self-control. The last thing he ever intended to do was hook up with a woman with a dangerous job, much less a client. He'd done it before and it had ended tragically. He wasn't about to risk that again.

Joelle was beautiful, intelligent and built like a pinup girl—which was exactly his type—and if she'd been an accountant and not his client, then he would have told Carter to come back in a couple of hours. But reality painted an entirely different picture and right now, he was thankful his friend had interrupted before he carried things too far.

"I'm glad you're here," Tyler said. "Joelle just got a call and texts that you need to see."

"From Brant?"

"It has to be." Tyler waved him toward the kitchen.

As he stepped inside, his gaze went immediately to Joelle. She stood in front of the refrigerator, drinking a bottled water, and a tiny blush crept up her face as he walked up to her.

"Hi, Carter," she said.

Tyler felt a pull of sympathy as she tried to force a smile, but didn't quite achieve it.

"Show him the texts," Tyler instructed.

She passed Carter the phone and they both watched as Carter scrolled through the feed. His jaw clenched tighter with every new image until Tyler wondered if his teeth would break. When he got to the last image, he cursed and placed the phone on the kitchen counter.

Tyler watched as Carter paced the length of the kitchen twice but wisely kept silent while his friend worked out his personal—and completely justified—anger.

Finally, Carter stopped pacing and ran one hand through his hair. "How is it that he's gotten all these photos in Calais and not a single person has seen him? I have every business owner and trustworthy person in town on the lookout. None of them have seen him."

He picked up the phone and scrolled to the picture of Alaina entering Johnny's Café. "These were taken on Main Street. How could he get close enough to take these pictures and yet no one saw him?"

"Maybe sitting in a vehicle with tinted windows?" Tyler suggested. "He could be farther away than we think and using a telephoto lens."

Carter scrolled to the picture taken at Willamina's house. "This one was taken from the property line, not thirty yards from where you were sitting. He could have easily picked you off with a rifle from that location."

"I don't think he wants to kill me," Joelle said. "If I'm dead, I can't tell him what he wants."

"No," Tyler said, "but he could kill one of your sisters to make you talk."

Carter blew out a breath and Tyler knew his friend had already gotten to that possibility.

Joelle's eyes widened and her jaw dropped. "I don't know why I'm surprised. I know he's capable of hurting someone, but I hoped the pictures were just to scare me."

"And they may be," Carter said, "but we can't assume that."

"Just out of curiosity," Tyler said, "but do you even know where Brant's wife is?"

Joelle shook her head. "It's one of the ways we protect the women. I deliver her to another person who delivers her to someone else. I have no idea how many hands she passes through before she arrives at a safe house. It's set up that way to protect the victims."

"And clearly it does," Tyler said, "but it doesn't

do much for the volunteers. Have you ever had something like this happen before?"

"Nothing like this. We've had husbands show up at the center where I work yelling threats, and a couple of them have grabbed me, but nothing ever escalated beyond that. Usually when the police get involved, they back off."

"Either Brant is supremely arrogant to think he won't get caught or he's not sane. This definitely escalated beyond simple threats."

Joelle's eyes filled with tears. "This is all my fault. I brought that monster to Calais and put my sisters in danger." Suddenly, she straightened up. "I'll leave. That will get Alaina and Danae out of danger."

"No." Tyler issued the directive without even thinking.

"Tyler's right," Carter said. "It wouldn't change anything. Brant is already aware of your sisters. He would still use them to get to you no matter where you go. What I don't understand is how he found out about them so quickly."

"He's smart," Joelle said. "Scary smart, and he has a whole fleet of private investigators at his fingertips. His wife showed us some of his records. He pays them a fortune and they'll do anything for him."

"It wouldn't be that hard to find out information about the estate," Tyler said. "Not if someone was looking."

Carter sighed. "No, probably not. So the question is, what can we do to protect them?"

"Yep," Tyler said, "and I'm up for any and all suggestions you have."

"Any luck on finding out how he's getting in the house?"

Tyler frowned. "No, and even worse, he knew the cameras were there. Gave me the one-finger wave when he went under the one in the entry."

Carter slammed his hand on the counter. "He's always one step ahead of us. Over two months I've been investigating and I'm no closer to knowing how now than I was then."

"That's not true," Tyler disagreed. "You've found out that Purcell was paying people for his dirty work, and you've already identified two of the Calais residents who were part of it. Granted, they're both dead, but two months ago, you didn't even know who Purcell really was, what he was up to and that anyone from Calais was involved."

"And despite two dead, I have to assume someone else from Calais is still in the thick of it," Carter said. "Someone knows their way around this house entirely too well."

"I've been over every room in here—both floors—and checked the windows and for any exterior passageway. They're all secure. With all the clutter, he could easily hide once inside, but I still have no idea how he's getting in."

"What about the attic?" Joelle asked. "Is there any way he could get in through the roof?"

Tyler shook his head. "I checked it first thing. The attic stairwell is at the end of the hall on the second floor above the laundry room, but I padlocked the door to it that day. No one is getting through there unless they can walk through walls."

"It almost seems like he can," Carter said.

"Do you want to take another look at everything?" Tyler asked. "Maybe if we go over it together, we'll think of something we haven't individually."

Carter threw his hands up in the air. "I'm willing to try anything. First, I want to call Alaina and Danae and give them a heads-up, and I'll need to borrow your phone, Joelle, so that I can forward this information to the Jackson police."

"Of course," Joelle said.

"Give me a minute," Carter said and stalked off toward the front of the house.

"What do you want me to do?" Joelle asked.

Tyler looked at her, then immediately shifted his gaze out the patio windows. With the taste of her cherry lip gloss still lingering on his lips, the question was one he couldn't answer honestly, especially as he didn't want to be honest with himself.

Finally, he looked back at her, trying to keep his thoughts on his job, where they belonged.

"I don't know. I mean, I guess do whatever you would have done otherwise—just carrying your pistol."

She sighed. "The real irony is I came here thinking I would avoid having to carry my pistol around inside my own house."

His heart ached for her, but he was glad Carter was just down the hall. If they were alone, he'd put his arms around her to comfort her, and he had a really good idea where that would go.

"We're going to figure this out."

She nodded, but he could tell she wasn't convinced. "I'm going to start sorting stuff in the downstairs rooms. I've spent a little time picking through it, but I need to start separating the good stuff from the garbage."

"I figure we'll start outside, so keep the doors locked and your phone on you as well as the pistol. I'm going to see if Carter is ready."

It took every ounce of control he had to leave her in the kitchen. It bothered him to see such a normally strong woman at the point of breaking, and it made him angry that evil men had put her in this position. He would figure out what was going on at the estate.

But he wasn't about to audition for the role of white knight. Not again.

HE WATCHED FROM his hiding place at the edge of the swamp. He'd seen the man and woman come out of the butler's pantry and made his call when he had a clear view of her through the kitchen patio windows. He wanted to see her response—her fear. He needed to remind her what he was capable of. She thought she already knew, but she had no idea. His bitch of a wife had no idea, but she would.

They both would, very soon.

JOELLE WATCHED AS Carter and Tyler exited the front door, and she locked it behind them. She checked her pistol for the third time that morning and slipped it into her waistband. Her cell phone was already tucked into her jeans pocket, so she headed into one of the back rooms to start digging through the stacks.

She'd already assembled some cardboard boxes that William had delivered and set them in the entry in different sections—keepsakes, donation, potential valuables and trash. She'd spent some time poking through stuff the previous days, but there was no way she could keep track of everything unless she started organizing it.

The first room she went in had a stack of boxes against the far wall and a chest of drawers against another wall. The closet looked as if it was going to spit its contents out onto the floor—assuming it could find a bit of open floor space.

She opened the first box and a flurry of dust flew up in her face. Coughing, she took a couple steps back and leaned against the wall. Who was she fooling? Her head wasn't in this. And despite her fear of Brant and absolute conviction that he was capable of hurting her or her sisters, her mind wasn't dwelling on him, either.

It was stuck on Tyler's kiss.

From the look on his face, she'd known it was coming, so it wasn't surprising on a momentary level. But now, after the fact, she was surprised that he'd ever gotten around to such a thing. At first, she'd thought Tyler didn't like her in the least, despite the fact that he didn't even know her. She could tell he resented her presence.

After talking to his father, she realized that his issues were internal, and he would have felt the same about anyone in her position. So it definitely wasn't personal, but it was still hard not to take his brusque attitude that way. Then when things intensified, he'd dropped the aggravated attitude and stepped instantly into professional mode, surprising her with an occasional bout of personal interaction. But even then, she was still well aware of the emotional wall he'd erected.

William thought Tyler had seen so many atrocities overseas that he needed time to decompress and work through them, and she was certain William was right. Given Tyler's specialty and the length of his time spent in a war zone, a certain level of PTSD should be expected.

But she'd always gotten the feeling that it was somehow more personal than that. That the wall he'd erected was specific to her, and not in place with his father or Carter. Maybe now, she knew the reason why. Clearly, Tyler was attracted to her. She hadn't mistaken his expression when he kissed her, but she'd understood his expression when Carter interrupted them, as well.

She wasn't surprised at the kiss, but he was.

He'd lost control—let down that wall for just a second and allowed her in, and that scared him so much that he'd fled when Carter interrupted. Seconds later, the wall was back in place, strong as ever and just as impenetrable.

Sighing, she pushed herself off the wall. She had no business dwelling on Tyler and his love life. He'd already made it clear that he didn't want to become involved and, realistically, it wasn't a good idea for her either. When all this was over, they would sell off the estate, dole out the money, and the sisters would continue the lives they'd already started. Now those lives would include one another, but Joelle didn't think for a moment that any of them were going to change directions simply because they'd found one another or become wealthy. All the money did was allow them to easily pursue things they'd always been working toward anyway.

And Tyler Duhon was not one of the things she'd been working toward.

Her mind said it; now, if only her body and heart would comply. Despite the standoffish attitude that was in place most of the time, Joelle was drawn to him in a way she never had been to another man, not even Brad. Tyler was an alpha male in every way, but she knew that beneath that bravado lay a kindness and empathy that made him even more attractive. She'd seen that side of him peek out a couple of times and knew that Tyler was so much deeper than the layers of absolutely perfect muscle that physically defined him.

When it came to the possibility of relationships, Tyler may as well be another ghost in the house— showing himself just enough to give her a taste of what he had to offer, but not sticking around long enough for her to touch something solid. Likely, he would remain that way the entire two weeks, then she would leave, and they would have polite exchanges when they happened to run into each other after that.

Depressing, but probably accurate.

Sighing, she reached into the box to lift out a stack of clothes, and then she heard the sound of glass breaking. Instantly, she froze, trying to figure out where the noise had originated. It sounded like it came from the direction of the kitchen.

She stepped out into the entry and listened again,

but only silence surrounded her. Maybe Carter and
Tyler came in the patio door and dropped something. She pulled her cell phone from her pocket,
then swore. The one bar of signal that had been
present earlier was gone.

She removed her pistol from her waistband and
headed for the kitchen, creeping down the hallway,
both hands clutching the pistol in front of her. She
stopped right before the entryway to the kitchen
and listened again, but no sound came from the
room. Maybe she'd been wrong. Maybe the noise
hadn't come from this direction at all.

She inched around the wall and peered into the
kitchen, but it was empty. Shaking her head, she
stepped around the corner, chastising herself for
creating a fright when there was no reason for one.

That's when he grabbed her.

He'd been standing against the wall right next to
the door just out of her field of vision when she'd
peered inside—in a perfect position to grab her
arms and shake the pistol loose. She screamed as
the pistol fell from her hands and slid across the
stone floor.

He yanked her around to face him and she stared
right into the face of the devil—Victor Brant. One
look at the .44 Magnum he held to her head and
the smile on his face, and her fear turned to terror.
This was it. She was going to die in this house at
the hands of a male abuser.

Just like her mother.

"Where is she?" he asked.

The calm politeness in his voice made her blood run cold. He wasn't human. At least, not in any of the good ways humans ought to be.

"I don't know where she is," she said.

His fingers dug into her arm and she winced. "Liar!"

Her heart pounded so hard in her chest that she thought it would break, but a sliver of anger replaced some of her fear. "I'm sure your flunkies looked into it. You know how this works. I passed her off. I don't know where she is."

His lips thinned and he narrowed his eyes at her. "You can find out. And you will."

Before she could reply, he pulled her into the butler's pantry.

"Open the trapdoor," he said.

She hesitated, trying to scramble for an escape plan.

He shoved the barrel of the gun into the back of her head so hard that her scalp ached. "Don't play dumb with me. I saw you go into the cellar with that man you're shacked up with. Had a real clear view through the patio windows."

She leaned over and pulled open the trapdoor.

"Get inside, and don't even think about fighting or I'll shoot you right here, then go after your sisters."

Everything she'd been taught told her to fight with her attacker and at least you leave a body that can be found—but what had her creeping down the stairs and into the cellar was her sisters. Brant was probably going to kill her, but maybe she could stall long enough for her sisters to get to safety. Carter had called them earlier to warn them. Surely, they were working out every possible precaution.

When they got to the bottom, Brant motioned her toward the tiny space under the stairs. "Get in there," he said.

She stepped in the cubby under the stairs, not even able to stand upright because of the low support beams, and looked back at Brant, her mind whirling with possibilities. What in the world was he going to do? If he killed her down here, it might take a long time for Tyler and Carter to find the body, and they would definitely go looking for her when they came inside and found her missing.

She cursed herself for her stupidity. The longer they spent looking for her, the more time it gave Brant to go after Alaina and Danae. When she'd come into the cellar, she'd thought she was buying her sisters time, but she'd forgotten that she was buying Brant time, as well.

Now she crouched there, waiting for the shot that would end it all—would destroy so many lives—but instead, he picked up a piece of plywood and propped it and covered the opening to the cubby.

With only a tiny bit of light streaming into the cellar from the butler's pantry, the cellar was already dim. But with the plywood covering the cubby, she was pitched into total darkness.

Chapter Fourteen

A wave of dizziness passed over Joelle as she heard Brant hammering the first nail into the plywood, and she struggled to keep from passing out. It wasn't a lack of air, as the steps and the opening had plenty of cracks, even with the plywood in place. It was fear. She took a deep breath and slowly blew it out, trying to keep herself from dwelling on the fact that he planned to leave her here, boarded up in this empty cellar.

Think! There has to be something you can do about it.

But what? Given her black belt, she could definitely kick and normally, the half-rotted piece of plywood in front of her wouldn't have taken her seconds to plow through, but crammed into a space where she couldn't even extend her legs made it impossible.

The hammering went on for what seemed an eternity, but finally, it stopped and she heard Brant breathing on the other side of the sealed opening.

"Give me what's mine," he said. "Or the next body I board up won't be breathing and it won't be yours. I'll give you some time to think about it."

A second later, she heard his footsteps above her, and then the trapdoor slammed shut. Panic coursed through her. For all intents and purposes, she'd been buried alive. The urge to scream was overwhelming, but she managed to choke it back. It would just use more air and energy, and she was too light-headed. Besides, she needed to save her strength to get out before Brant could get to Alaina and Danae.

She turned sideways and placed her shoulder against the plywood, then leaned away from it as far as possible and slammed her shoulder into the wood. Pain shot through her arm and up her neck, but the plywood didn't budge. She took a deep breath and tried again. The wood bent out a bit, but she didn't hear a single splinter. Nerves in her shoulder set off, sending shock waves that felt like fire shooting down her arm. Involuntarily, she grabbed her arm and squeezed it, trying to stop the pain from moving farther down, but it moved right past her grip and into her hand.

Brant had secured the plywood well. Too well. And she couldn't get her leg in place for a good kick without risking breaking her ankle or foot.

He'd won.

He'd closed her off from her protectors, both of

whom were here with her instead of protecting her sisters. And that was the part that bothered her the most.

She slumped against the wall and slid down until she collapsed on the dirt floor. There was nothing left to do now but cry.

TYLER OPENED THE front door and punched in a code for the alarm. He and Carter had spent almost an hour inspecting every square inch of the outside of the house—banging on it with hammers, poking at it with pry bars—and digging through the brush surrounding the house for signs of passage. They'd come up with exactly nothing.

"You want something to drink?" Tyler asked.

"I'd love a whole bottle of scotch or a case of beer," Carter replied, "but that won't help us find answers. I'll settle for water or soda, if you've got it."

"I'm out of ideas as to how else he'd get in," Tyler said. "Unless he's living inside the house and never left, I've got nothing."

"Yeah. I do think someone was in here while Danae was working in the house. They had to have overheard conversations we had in order to make the moves they did. But I always assumed the front door was the weak link. You've eliminated that possibility with the alarm."

"We're missing something," Tyler said as he stepped into the kitchen. His shoes crunched on something and he stopped, staring down at the broken glass that littered the floor.

"Where's Joelle?" Tyler asked, his pulse ticking up a notch. "Did you see her in the entry when we came in?"

Carter frowned. "No, and I didn't hear her either, which is strange. You'd think she would have come out to talk to us when she heard you turning off the alarm."

"Joelle!" Tyler yelled, trying to keep from panicking. "Something's wrong. No way Joelle would leave broken glass all over the floor."

"Maybe she cut her hand and went upstairs to clean it off," Carter suggested.

Desperate to cling to any normal and safe explanation, Tyler nodded, even though it didn't feel right. "I'll check," he said and dashed into the servants' staircase in the kitchen.

Taking the stairs two at a time, he prayed that Joelle was upstairs, wrapping a bandage around her finger. He burst out into the upstairs hallway and yelled Joelle's name again before looking in her bedroom. Empty. He ran to the hallway bathroom as Carter stepped out of the stairwell.

"It's empty," he said to Carter, panic now setting in full force.

Carter immediately sized up the situation. "Whatever went down started in the kitchen. Let's go back there and figure out where to start looking."

Tyler nodded and ran back downstairs. People didn't disappear without a trace. They would find something to help them track Joelle.

If it wasn't too late.

Tyler pushed that thought from his mind. He had to focus on the mission. He couldn't afford to start thinking of the potential costs. Or casualties. He rushed into the kitchen and this time went around the counter to avoid stepping in the glass. Carter was right behind him.

At the edge of the counter, Tyler bent over and picked through the glass. "The bottom of the glass is here, which is probably where it broke. It scattered evenly in all directions, so it was probably dropped rather than thrown."

"I agree," Carter said. "Was any of the glass tracked outside of the splatter?"

"Yeah, toward the servants' staircase, but that could have been me."

"Nothing else? Joelle is wearing tennis shoes. They wouldn't pick up the glass like our boots."

Tyler leaned farther over until his face was only inches from the floor, looking for even a glint of light reflecting off of glass. His heart fell as he covered foot after foot of the stone floor without a single spec of glass. Then something caught his eye—a tiny shard several feet away.

"That way," he said, pointing toward the breakfast nook. "Only a single piece but well outside of the range it would have scattered from the drop."

Tyler walked to where the shard lay and checked again, but this time, he couldn't locate another piece of glass. "Nothing else," he said and glanced across the breakfast nook.

"Wait!" He jumped up and hurried over to the dark object underneath the table. His heart leaped into his throat as he reached under the table and drew out Joelle's pistol. He held the gun up to Carter, whose eye's widened.

"Damn it!" Carter said and stepped over to the patio door. "It's open, and the storm's moving in. We won't have light for much longer."

"Start trying to find tracks," Tyler said. "I'll grab some flashlights."

Tyler ran to the butler's pantry where they'd left the flashlights earlier. He grabbed them from the counter, but when he turned to leave, his boot hung on the rug. Drawing up short, he stared down at the ugly, rumpled rug, certain he'd left it flat and even.

He looked out the patio windows where Carter was disappearing into the brush just off the kitchen. He should be out there, but something kept him from moving. It would only take a minute to make sure no one was down there.

Before he could change his mind, he yanked open the door and ran down the stairs, shining his flashlight across the black room. Nothing. Disappointed, he turned to leave and his light flashed across the stairs. He froze, certain that piece of plywood had not been nailed up there before.

"Joelle," he called out.

"Tyler!" Joelle cried out as she started banging on the plywood. "Get me out of here!"

The sheer panic in her voice launched his anger into the stratosphere. He dropped the flashlight and grabbed a pry bar from the tools in the corner, attacking the plywood with everything he had. It only took two pushes before the plywood splintered and popped off the framing.

He threw the plywood on the floor and reached out as Joelle leaped into his arms. Her entire body was shaking and he worried that she would go into shock.

"Are you hurt?" he asked.

"No," she whispered between sobs.

He held her tightly, overwhelmed with relief that she was safe, mixed with insurmountable anger at what Brant had done to her.

"Let's get out of here," he said when the sobs finally wound down a bit. "Carter went outside looking for you."

She sniffed but allowed him to pull back from her. Her face was puffy and her eyes bloodshot, but she didn't appear to have any physical injuries. Tyler knew, though, that the emotional ones were harder to overcome.

"Can you walk?" he asked.

She nodded.

"You go first. I'll be right behind you." He fell in step close behind her. She was a little shaky walking up the stairs, but he was right there if she started to fall.

She crawled out of the trapdoor and slumped onto the pantry floor. He climbed out and reached down to help her into the kitchen, where he sat her in a chair. The clean laundry still sat folded at the end of the breakfast table, and he grabbed a blanket and wrapped it around her.

"I don't want you to go into shock," he said. "Keep this wrapped around you."

He pulled her pistol from his waistband and placed it on the table in front of her. Gripping her shoulders with both hands, he leaned over and looked her straight in the eyes. "I've got to go outside and get Carter."

"Hurry," she whispered.

He ran outside and down to the end of the patio where he'd seen Carter enter the swamp, yelling out his name. A couple seconds later, he heard someone running through the foliage, then Carter burst through a drapery of vines and skidded to a stop on the patio.

"Inside," Tyler said and hurried back inside, Carter right on his heels.

Tyler locked the patio door behind them and gave

Carter a rundown of how he'd found Joelle. Carter knelt beside her and took her hand in his.

"Are you all right?"

"Yes, but you have to go!" Joelle straightened up in her chair and Tyler could practically feel the tension rolling off of her. "It was Brant. He said he'd go after Alaina and Danae. You have to protect them."

Carter pulled out his cell phone and cursed when he saw there was no signal.

"Go," Tyler said. "I'm going to get Joelle to Doc Broussard. If the cell phones don't work in town, I'll call dispatch from Doc's office and arrange a place to meet up."

Carter was already halfway across the kitchen before Tyler even finished speaking.

"I don't need the doctor," Joelle said.

"That's not your call to make, it's mine. I know you have a lot of experience with crisis, but you're usually on the other side of the desk, so no arguing. Besides, do you have any idea what my dad would do to me if I didn't get you medical attention?"

Although it was the truth, he'd said it to make her smile, and he gave her credit for the effort. He extended his hand down to her and helped her up from the chair. She was still a bit unsteady, but she no longer shivered, which was a good sign.

"Do you have service yet?" Joelle asked as they exited the house.

He checked his cell phone display. "No, but I

promise I'll check in with everyone when we get to Doc Broussard's."

Joelle nodded and wrapped her arms across her chest. She seemed steadier, but she was so pale, and although Tyler wanted to make sure nothing was physically wrong with her, he was more worried about her mental health.

No matter what, they had a long night ahead of them.

Chapter Fifteen

Carter paced from one end of the sheriff's department office to the other so many times, he thought he'd wear a hole in the old carpet. Alaina perched on the end of the lobby couch, exchanging glances with Thelma, the gray-headed dispatcher.

"What?" he asked on his tenth pass, as Alaina looked at him, eyebrows raised.

"We're just wondering whether to get you a drink or extra bullets, or perhaps call for new flooring."

He threw his arms up in the air. "Hell if I know. I've never been at such a loss. I'd tell all of you to get out of here and go to Mexico, but Brant won't stop there. He'd just move on to me or Zach or Tyler or even worse, William or my mother."

"You think it's that bad?" Alaina asked.

"He dragged Joelle into the cellar and boarded her into a wall while Tyler and I were right outside. A cellar with one exit, and he took the time to nail plywood in place. We could have walked in at any minute and he'd have been trapped down there. That's not sane."

"No, it's not," Alaina agreed. "But what do we do? I'll bet I've been through every possible solution you have, including having all of us move in to that blasted house until this is over."

"He'd just launch a stick of dynamite through a window and get us all."

She sighed. "I got around to that, too. Face it, Carter, the best thing we can do is what we're already doing. Stay put and stay aware. Did you find how Brant got in the house?"

"I didn't even take the time to look. I was too worried about getting word to you and Danae and I had no signal, as usual."

"The caretaker's cabin and the rental cabin are still uninhabitable, right?"

"Yeah. Zach hasn't had time to address them at all, and his crew can only get so much work done over the weekend. With all the problems at the main house, I don't think they've done anything on the cabins."

"So Joelle has to stay in the main house or leave and start her two weeks again some other time. Maybe that's what needs to happen. Maybe she needs to get out of Calais long enough for you to find the entry point."

"No," Joelle's voice sounded in the doorway and

Carter whipped around as Alaina jumped up from the couch and rushed over to hug her sister.

"Sit," Alaina insisted and guided Joelle to the couch. "What did Doc Broussard say?"

"He says I'm lucky," Joelle said, her voice breaking a bit. "I was in a bit of shock when I got there, but he gave me a shot of something and a bottle of something else."

Alaina nodded. "Antianxiety meds, probably. Don't be afraid to take them. You, of all people, know how difficult this is going to be for you to process. Promise me, you will take your own advice when it comes to taking care of yourself."

Joelle's eyes misted up and she leaned over to hug Alaina. "I promise," she said as she released her.

Alaina leaned back and narrowed her eyes. "What's wrong with your shoulder? You're holding your arm funny."

"I tried to break down the plywood. It's not dislocated or anything but Doc Broussard said it's going to be black and blue by tomorrow. It's pretty sore."

Alaina rose from the couch and grabbed her purse from the dispatcher's desk. "You guys catch up on everything. I'm going to run to the general store and pick up an ice pack and a heating pad. You'll need both. I'll be back in a sec."

"Alaina," Carter said, and she paused in the doorway. "Be careful."

She gave him a single nod before hurrying outside.

"So what's the plan?" Tyler asked.

Carter shook his head. "I've alerted the Jackson police and the state police, but neither of them have the manpower to send backup—at least, not until next week. So we're on our own until then. If you want to leave—"

"I don't," Joelle interrupted. "Location is irrelevant. I'd rather stay where I'm surrounded by people who care about me."

"Good," Carter said. "I wish there were other options for living quarters, but if you want to meet the inheritance requirements, you're going to have to stay in the main house. After that last storm blew through, neither of the cabins is fit for living."

"Don't worry," Tyler said. "I have some ideas about securing the house, at least at night. And from this point forward, Joelle will not be leaving my sight."

"I have to shower," Joelle said with a small smile.

"Then I'll be standing outside the bathroom door with my pistol…or two."

"And my first day here, you said it wouldn't come to that."

Carter smiled. "Think you can put that 24/7 guard plan on hold for thirty minutes or so?"

"Why?"

"I'd like to have another chat with Bert Thibodeaux. I still think he knows more than he's telling me, and maybe if we explain that assault and kidnapping could be part of the deal, he'll give something up."

"And why do you want me there?"

"A second set of eyes. I've missed the boat so many times on this mess that I'm starting to second-guess myself."

Tyler looked over at Joelle, the hesitation on his face clear as day.

"Go," Joelle urged. "I'll be fine. I'm sitting in the sheriff's office in broad daylight. I couldn't get safer if I tried."

He studied her a couple seconds more, then Thelma stood up behind the dispatcher's desk and pumped a sawed-off 12-gauge.

"Don't worry," she said with a broad smile. "I got you covered."

"Is that even legal?" Tyler asked.

Carter patted him on the back. "I didn't see a thing."

TYLER WAS LOST in thought on the drive to Bert's place, trying to put together all the pieces and at the same time, formulate a plan to ensure that Brant—or anyone else—didn't get to Joelle. It was all jumbled together in his mind, and every avenue of thought he started down led to a dead end or more questions.

Finally, he sighed and looked over at Carter. "I understand why you've been so frustrated over all of this. I mean, I thought I understood before, but now…"

Carter nodded. "In all my years as a detective in New Orleans, I never had a case with so many moving pieces, and so many hidden ones. And never a crime that stretched back twenty-five years, implicating people along the way."

Tyler shook his head. "It's impossible to determine what's happening because of Brant and what's happening because of Purcell."

"It's always been that way. With Alaina, at first, I thought everything was about the estate, and I was wrong. With Danae, at first, I thought she might have brought trouble with her, and I was wrong. Now I'm sure it's both, but it doesn't put me any closer to catching Brant or exposing the rest of Purcell's crew, much less their intentions."

"And you think Bert is part of Purcell's crew?"

"I know he was insofar as he was one of Purcell's errand boys. He picked up the valuables Purcell bought with estate funds, then hauled them back to New Orleans for sale. Purcell promised him a new rig when he died, but Bert got screwed on that like everyone else Purcell made promises to. Bert tries to claim ignorance on anything beyond his trucking service, but I've always thought he was lying. He thinks Purcell owes him, and he's definitely capable of trying to collect after the fact."

"So you think he knows something, but the question is, what? And is it relevant to anything else we're worried about?"

"Exactly."

Carter pulled his truck up in front of Bert's cabin and parked it behind the man's semi. "His pickup truck's here," Carter said. "That's a good sign."

They walked to the front door and Carter pounded on it a few times. "Open up, Bert. It's Sheriff Trahan."

Nothing stirred inside and Carter frowned. "Look in that window and see if you see anything."

Tyler walked over to one of the front windows and attempted to peer inside. The dirt and grime cut the field of vision, but he got a decent view of the man's living room. "Looks like a pigsty."

"Yeah, I got a peek around last time I talked to him. He's not winning any awards for housekeeping."

"There's a red lace bra hanging from a lamp." He straightened up and shook his head. "Some women really have no taste at all."

Carter laughed. "Clearly."

"Maybe he's fishing," Tyler said. "That pier doesn't look in much better shape than his house, but it's probably good enough for a boat launch."

"Yes, probably so," Carter said and pounded on the door one last time. Finally, he sighed. "I'll try again later."

As they turned to walk away, the door flew open and Bert glared at them.

"Waking me up is getting to be a habit with you, Sheriff," Bert said, his scorn clear when he said the word *sheriff.*

Carter gave him a fake smile. "I don't want to be here any more than you want me here."

"Then why don't you do us both a favor and stop coming." He started to close the door, but Carter put his hand on the door to stop him.

"It's not that easy, Bert. I got problems in Calais, and I think you know something about them."

Bert crossed his arms over his chest and smirked. "That right. Let me guess, you got another rich bitch on your hands whining about keeping her and her money safe."

A rush of anger passed through Tyler and he itched to punch the man right in his smug jaw.

"What I've got," Carter said, "is a stalker, a kidnapper and someone who breaks into houses and assaults women."

"Sounds like a real problem. Maybe you should stop hassling me and do something about it."

"I am doing something about it. Any of those descriptions fit you?"

Something flickered in Bert's eyes, but it was gone as quickly as it appeared. Bert dropped his hands. "Look, I already told you all I did for Purcell was cart stuff up and down the highway to New

Orleans. I don't know nothing about kidnappings and beating up on women, especially rich bitches."

"Who says the assault was on a rich woman?"

"Please. Everyone in Calais knows the sheriff's department works for the LeBeau sisters."

Tyler glanced at Bert's shack. "A woman with money might come in handy."

"Yeah," Bert said. "That worked out well for Purcell. Don't worry about me. I make my own money."

"Like Roger and Jack?" Carter asked. "Making money the Purcell way got them killed. If you know anything about that, you need to tell me now."

Bert sneered. "You afraid I'm in danger, Sheriff?"

"Maybe."

"Well, don't worry your pretty little head about it. I can take care of myself."

He stepped back and slammed the door.

"I see what you mean," Tyler said as they climbed into Carter's truck.

"He's hiding something, right?"

"Yeah. I'd bet on it. But we already know Victor Brant, not Bert, attacked Joelle."

Carter nodded. "But did you see his look when I mentioned the assault?"

"It bothered him, but I can't figure why."

Carter sighed. "I can't help thinking if we knew

the answer to that question, we'd be halfway to solving all of this."

Tyler looked at Bert's cabin in the passenger's mirror as they drove away and saw curtains on the kitchen window slide back into place. It was clear to Tyler that Bert was nervous about something. He only hoped Carter figured out what it was before someone else wound up dead.

JOELLE PULLED THE T-shirt over her head, wincing as she lifted her right arm up and caught sight of it in the mirror. It was throbbing a little and she could see a light purple shade was already setting in on it. By tomorrow, she had no doubt it'd look like her entire biceps had been caught in a vise.

She pulled her wet hair back with a clip, not about to bother with a blow-dryer, and slipped her feet into flip-flops. When she pulled open the bathroom door, she drew up short for a second, then remembered that the armed man standing outside the door was Tyler.

"Sorry," he said as he caught sight of her. "I didn't mean to startle you."

She waved a hand in dismissal. "I knew you were out here. I don't know why I'm so jumpy."

"Don't you?"

She sighed. "I guess those meds aren't doing much."

"They're doing enough. We don't want you drugged beyond the point of reaction."

The thought of being so out of it she couldn't move and wouldn't even care held a sliver of appeal, but Joelle knew Tyler was right. She had to be able to run or fight or whatever else may be called for.

"What about you?" she asked.

"What do you mean?"

"I assume you'd like to take a shower. How do you intend to do that if you're not letting me out of your sight?"

"I've been thinking about that. I know this will be uncomfortable for you, but I thought I'd put a chair in the bathroom. You can sit with your back to the shower."

She stared. "You want me to sit in the bathroom with you while you shower? Are you going to shower with your gun?"

"No, but there's a shelf at shoulder height right outside the shower. It will be within easy reach."

A million reasons why this was a horrible idea ran through her mind. A million reasons to choose from and all she had to do was select one.

"That's okay," he said. "I'll just wait until tomorrow when Carter can guard you."

Great. Now she felt guilty. Tyler had spent half the day tromping around the swamp, with unseasonably warm temperatures and humidity that made you sweat indoors, much less outside. She wasn't about to send him to bed dirty, itchy and sweaty.

"Fine," she said. "I'll file my nails or something."

"Thanks," he said, and the grateful look he gave her made her feel guilty for hesitating.

He dragged a small chair from one of the bedrooms into the bathroom, then squeezed by to the shower. "Close the door and lock it," he instructed as he pulled her pistol from his waistband and handed it to her.

She closed and locked the door, then pulled the chair up a bit to allow him more room to undress. The bathroom was tiny, and with the two of them and the chair, the floor space was almost gone. She set her gun on the edge of the sink, next to the chair, and grabbed her makeup bag.

"Ready when you are," she called out as she slid onto the chair, her back to the shower.

The water came on, and then she heard the sound of clothes falling on the tile floor. She pulled her nail file from her makeup bag, trying to force her mind from thinking about Tyler and his perfect chest and back. Then she heard a zipper and knew he'd removed his jeans. She'd bet the entire LeBeau estate that his legs were just as impressive as everything else on him.

Her compact rested at the top of her makeup bag—almost daring her to take it out and open it up. She shoved it to the bottom of the bag, chastising herself for high school thoughts, but couldn't stop the sliver of disappointment she felt at her lack of adventure. Sighing, she began to file her nails.

She was about to spend the entire night in a twin bed not two feet away from the man. The last thing she needed was to go to bed with a clear mental picture of exactly what rested beneath those covers.

When Tyler had told her they would be sharing a room from this point forward, she'd protested, but his argument was sound. The patio off her bedroom was a security risk. It was smarter to move into Tyler's room, which had no patio and only one window with no trees offering access. The problem was, Tyler's room was tiny—maybe ten by ten—and even though she had a separate bed, they were so close that she may as well be sleeping alongside him.

Still, although she'd never admit it, she did feel safer knowing he would be so close she could reach out and touch him. He'd placed her bed against the wall on the opposite side of the door. If anyone came inside, they'd have to go through Tyler to get to her. Of course, if she wanted to go to the restroom in the middle of the night, she'd have to practically climb over him to get out.

The thought of climbing over Tyler led to a whole other set of images, and she bent her file against her finger and it flicked over her shoulder. She leaned over and felt the floor behind her, still facing the door, and finally, her fingertips touched the edge of the elusive board. She leaned over a tiny bit farther to get her fingers on top of it and realized too late that she'd completely miscalculated her balance.

The chair tipped a tiny bit to the side, then the legs slid across the tile floor, sweeping the chair out from under her.

Chapter Sixteen

Joelle crashed onto the floor, groaning as her left shoulder hit the hard tile. Great, now she'd have two purple arms tomorrow. She could wear a muscle shirt and double as Barney.

In the excitement of the fall, she didn't realize that the shower had shut off, but now the quiet of the bathroom seemed to echo around her. She closed her eyes for a second, wondering what in the world she'd done to deserve this.

Just get up and stand in the corner until he's dressed.

That sounded reasonable, so she opened her eyes, preparing to rise, and a giant foot appeared in front of her.

"Are you all right?"

Tyler's voice sounded above her and she held in another groan. Her mortification hadn't been this high since she'd ripped her gym shorts during square-dancing class in eighth grade.

"I'm fine," she managed.

"Let me help you up."

The "No" was still on the tip of her tongue when his hands slid under her arms and he pulled her straight up to a standing position. She clenched her eyes again, praying that when she opened them, she would find it had all been a really bad dream.

"You can open your eyes," he said. "I'm wearing a towel."

Definitely not a dream.

She opened one eye and saw him standing directly in front of her, wearing nothing but a towel and a sexy grin.

"If I'd known sitting in the bathroom could be so dangerous, I would have gotten you shoulder pads."

"I dropped my fingernail file," she said, cringing inwardly at how incredibly lame she sounded.

"And the potential of seeing me naked was so horrible that you risked breaking your arm instead?"

"No…I mean…I…" She clamped her mouth shut, unable to fathom any response that didn't implicate her one way or another.

He stepped closer to her and she could feel the heat coming off of his skin. A flush ran through her from head to toe as an overwhelming desire to touch his bare chest came over her. Then he lowered his lips to hers and all apprehension melted away. Lost in his kiss, she ran her hand across his chest, feeling every square inch of his perfectly toned body.

He put his arms around her and pulled her body next to his. That's when she realized his towel had slipped to the floor, and the reality of being pressed against his completely naked body sent a chill through her. Moving his lips from hers, he trailed kisses down her neck and she moaned.

Then without warning, he swept her up in his arms and carried her out of the bathroom and into the bedroom, where he placed her on one of the twin beds. She looked up at him, marveling at his physique. Even the scars that graced his skin made him more masculine, more attractive.

"Protection?" she asked, praying that he had some.

He nodded and reached into a nightstand for his wallet. While he was otherwise engaged, she shrugged off her T-shirt, yoga pants and undies. Her body trembled as he moved into position over her, lowering his lips to hers again. He entered her in one fluid motion and she gasped, digging her fingernails into the soft skin of his shoulders.

Her body felt as if it were on fire, starting at her center and flaming out through every square inch of her. She clutched his back and moaned as he set the pace. The last thing she could remember thinking before he sent them both over the edge was how much she wished this moment would never end.

THE TINY BED didn't leave much room for two grown adults, but Joelle didn't mind the narrow space one bit. Her body pressed against Tyler's, their hot, bare skin touching from head to toe. Satisfied as she'd never been before, she laid her head on his chest and closed her eyes, relishing the moment.

"I didn't want to get involved with you," Tyler said quietly.

"I know."

"You did?"

She looked up at him and smiled. "You don't exactly do subtle."

"No," he said with a laugh. "I guess I don't."

"You plan on telling me why, or are you still keeping secrets?"

He ran his fingers across her hair and sighed. "There are things I've experienced that I don't plan on ever telling anyone, but since this one sort of involves you, I guess I can give you the basics."

Joelle pushed herself up on her elbow so that she could look directly at him, surprised he'd agreed so easily. "I'd love to hear anything you want to share, and I promise not to push for more."

He nodded. "There was a woman—a specialist in my line of work—that I met on my third tour of duty. She was brilliant and beautiful, and I was a little surprised when she wanted me."

"I'm not surprised."

He smiled and leaned over to kiss her, then straightened back up, and his smile faded. "Unfortunately, she took risks. Don't get me wrong—it was our job to take risks, but she took it to a whole other level. A level that put her in more danger than she needed to be. Our commander came up with an idea. It was far-fetched but if it worked, it would have given us a huge tactical advantage."

"You didn't want to do it."

He shook his head. "It went against protocol and all good common sense, but she was enthralled with the idea of gaining such an upper hand. I tried to talk her out of it, but she was already invested. So I agreed to partner with her as security detail."

Before he even said the words, Joelle knew what they would be. Her heart fell as he took in a deep breath and stared up at the ceiling. Finally, he looked back down at her.

"We walked into a trap. In a matter of seconds, I was living my worst fear."

The pain in his eyes was so clear that her heart

ached for him. She placed her hand on his chest. "I'm so sorry," she said.

"I couldn't save her. It was my job to keep her safe, and I failed."

"It wasn't your failure," she said, although she knew he wasn't ready to accept that. "You were against the mission from the beginning. If they had listened to you…"

"I shouldn't have agreed to go."

"Would that have prevented her from going?"

He sighed. "No."

"Then there's nothing you could have done, but I understand how much that bothers you, truly I do."

He nodded. "I guess you probably do."

"It's an awful feeling…to see something horrible coming and not be able to change it. You're constantly internally screaming at people to give you control so that you can save them."

"But people rarely do."

"No."

"How do you keep doing it? Keep trying to help people when you know so many of them are already lost?"

She shook her head. "I guess I focus on the ones we save."

"Yeah," he said, but she could tell he wasn't convinced. "Anyway, that's why I avoided getting involved with you. I didn't want to care for someone who voluntarily put herself in a position of danger, and your job definitely qualifies."

"I understand," she said, "but I'm glad you changed your mind."

She moved closer to kiss him and he wrapped his arms around her, pulling her naked body against his. And within minutes, he began the slow pace that would send them both over the edge again.

TYLER PULLED ON his jeans the next morning, looking down at Joelle, who was still asleep in the narrow bed they'd shared. Shared, and darn near destroyed if his ego was to be believed. He'd been attracted to her from the moment he laid eyes on her, but even his imagination hadn't come close to what it had been like to make love to her. And that was saying a lot, given that he had a fairly good imagination.

She stirred and looked up at him with a lazy smile. "What time is it?"

"Almost eight o'clock. We slept late."

"Well, most of the night wasn't about sleeping…."

He laughed as he sat next to her and leaned over to give her a kiss. "Well, there is that. How's your arm?"

"Which one?"

He smiled, fondly remembering her tumble onto the bathroom floor. After all, it had kicked off the best night of his entire life. "Both."

She glanced down. "Stiff and certainly not the most attractive, but not as bad as I thought they'd be." She reached up to touch his face with her hand. "I'm glad you changed your mind about dangerous women."

He shrugged. "I cheated, really. I mean, once the Brant issue is solved, you're free and clear. Your two weeks will end and you'll get the mother lode of cash from the estate. You can spend the rest of your life doing anything you want—reading, traveling…spending sleepless nights with security experts."

Her smile slipped away and she sat up. "I…I'm not planning on quitting my job."

"Sure you will. Your job's in Jackson and your family is here. Besides, you won't have to work, much less at something so difficult and dangerous."

"It's true…I have already thought about moving closer to Alaina and Danae. We have so many lost years to make up for and it will be easier if I'm close. But, Tyler, you have to know I don't have any intention of leaving my profession. I want to help women. What I do makes a difference."

Tyler jumped up from the bed and practically ran from the room. "This was a mistake."

Before he'd even made it to the doorway, the tears spilled over Joelle's cheeks.

Chapter Seventeen

Tyler dropped Joelle off at the general store and watched as she walked inside with Alaina before heading down the sidewalk for the café. The ride into Calais had been silent and uncomfortable, and he welcomed an hour away from Joelle and all the problems she brought with her.

He slid onto a stool at the café without even looking at Carter. He waved a finger and Sonia slid a cup of coffee in front of him, then wisely set off across the café with her pot and her smile. Clearly, she understood that the smile part would be wasted here.

"Women trouble?" Carter asked.

Tyler choked on his coffee and Carter slapped his back.

"Everyone says your mom is psychic," Tyler said once he could breathe properly. "Did you inherit the ability?"

"You don't need to be psychic to know that look. I've worn it myself."

"Women troubles? You?"

"Hey, I'm engaged to a LeBeau sister. Do I have to say more?"

Tyler took another drink of his coffee. "Clearly, you and Zach got the rational sisters. I got stuck with the stubborn one who won't listen to reason."

"Oh, man." Carter laughed. "You really don't know Alaina very well, do you? I'm not going to speak for Danae because I'm not the man sleeping with her, but I'm going to go out on a limb and guess that Zach would find that statement as amusing as I do."

"I… Who said I was sleeping with her?"

"Dude, you don't care how stubborn they are unless you're sleeping with them. So what kind of 'reasonable' advice did you give Joelle that she's not interested in taking?"

"I suggested she change careers because the one she has now is too dangerous."

"Whooooooo, boy, you've put your foot into it big-time."

"What's wrong with wanting her to be safe? Or, for that matter, what's wrong with my not wanting to be involved with a woman who has a dangerous job?"

"Asks the guy who's starting a security firm."

Tyler frowned. "I'm not going to do fieldwork. I'm going to run the company and work with hardware."

"Uh-huh."

Tyler threw his hands in the air. "You sound just like my dad."

"William's a smart man."

Tyler huffed, then looked over at a grinning Carter. Unable to help himself, he smiled.

"I'm not trying to give you a hard time," Carter said. "I know how it feels to be at odd ends career-wise, not really sure what you even want for a future, and then to have it all clouded with stalkers and an incredible woman. I met Alaina at the time of my life when I knew less about myself and what I wanted than I ever had."

"Then how did you know you were supposed to be with her?"

"Because no matter what future I imagined for myself, I couldn't come up with one where she wasn't in it."

Tyler forced his mind to imagine himself five years from now—running a successful security firm, with a little cabin on the bayou somewhere in Calais, maybe a golden retriever. Then the door to the cabin opened and Joelle stepped out.

"Crap," he said.

Carter clapped him on the back. "The bar's not open for several hours. Let me buy you breakfast."

As he waved for Sonia, Carter's cell phone rang. He glanced at the display and frowned. "Carter," he answered.

Tyler watched his friend's face as it grew tight, his jaw flexing. Something was wrong.

"I've got to cancel breakfast," Carter said.

"What's wrong?"

Carter glanced around the café, then lowered his voice. "A fisherman pulled a body out of the east side bayou."

Tyler sat up straight. "Who is it?"

"The fisherman didn't recognize him." Carter studied Tyler for a moment. "Joelle's with Alaina, right?"

"Yeah, they're picking out paint or something over at the general store."

"I'll call Alaina and tell her to stick close and stay in Calais. If you don't mind, I'd like you to come with me."

"Sure," Tyler hopped off the stool and tossed some money on the counter for the coffee before hurrying out after Carter.

If the fisherman didn't recognize the body, that meant one of two things—either it was too badly damaged to identify or it was someone the fisherman didn't know, such as Victor Brant.

Tyler hoped for option number two.

As JOELLE AND Alaina wrapped up their paint shopping and made their way out of the general store, Alaina's cell phone rang. As soon as she answered, Joelle could see a shift in her sister's demeanor, but Joelle couldn't extrapolate the problem from only

Alaina's end of the conversation. By the time she hung up the phone, Alaina was frowning.

"What's wrong?"

"That was Carter. He said there's something he needs to check out and he's taking Tyler with him. He wants me to stay with you and says neither of us should return to the estate without them."

"He didn't say what they were doing?"

"No, but I could tell he was worried by the sound of his voice."

Joelle shook her head. "Maybe they're checking up on a suspect. I'm sure they'll let us know as soon as they finish."

"I'm sure you're right. Come on. We may as well kill some time over coffee."

Joelle slid into the corner booth at the café across from Alaina, trying to maintain her composure, even though her heart was completely broken and her pride was annihilated. So far, she'd managed to keep Alaina from figuring out something was bothering her, and that was fairly impressive given Alaina's track record as a trial attorney.

They had no sooner slid into the booth than a pretty young woman stepped up to them with a pad of paper.

"'Morning, Alaina," she said.

"Good morning, Sonia," Alaina replied and waved a hand at Joelle. "This is my sister Joelle."

Sonia smiled. "Guess this means you're all here now. That's nice. Can I get you some breakfast?"

"I'll just have coffee for now," Joelle managed.

"Me, too," Alaina chimed in.

Alaina glanced back as Sonia walked away, then looked over at Joelle. "You going to tell me what's bothering you? Please don't make me work for it. I didn't sleep all that well."

"Me, either."

Alaina gave her a sympathetic look. "Are you too stressed staying in the house?"

"Yes, I'm stressed, but that's not it." Joelle paused as Sonia pushed cups of coffee in front of them. "I saw something that first night I stayed in the house. I didn't say anything to anyone, but Tyler got it out of me."

Alaina nodded. "Tyler told Carter and Carter told me."

"He said you and Danae saw things, too."

Alaina dumped some sweetener in her coffee and stirred. "By things, do you mean our mother's ghost?"

"Is there more than one?" Joelle tried to joke, but her delivery lacked enthusiasm.

"Yes, actually," Alaina said, completely serious. "I saw two different spirits. One was definitely Mother. Danae saw her, too."

"And the other?"

Alaina shook her head. "It didn't look like anyone, but it felt like pure evil."

Joelle sucked in a breath. "Purcell?" she whispered.

"That's what I think."

"Wow. I hope I don't see him. I don't even like remembering him."

Alaina frowned. "I can't remember much about him at all. Things about us girls and Mom are coming back, but Purcell is always like a shadow—like he's offstage when I'm remembering. Is that how it is for you?"

Joelle shook her head. "Unfortunately, no. Some of my memories of Purcell are very vivid, and none of them are pleasant."

Alaina reached across the table and squeezed Joelle's hand.

"Well, isn't this a pretty picture?" A man's voice boomed beside them.

Joelle looked up at a beefy man, probably in his sixties, who smiled down at them.

"Mayor Dupree," Alaina acknowledged. "Have you met my sister Joelle yet?"

The mayor extended his hand to Joelle. "I should have known such a lovely young lady was one of Ophelia's girls. It's a pleasure to meet you."

Joelle shook his hand and studied his face. "Nice to meet you, as well," she said.

"Is something wrong?" the mayor asked as he released her hand.

"No." Joelle realized she'd been staring. "I'm sorry. It's just that you look familiar, but I can't imagine when I would have seen you before."

"Oh, well, Johnny's my brother. Some say we favor each other, so that's probably it."

Joelle glanced over at the café owner, but didn't really see much resemblance.

"I didn't know Johnny was your brother," Alaina said. "Carter really needs to do a better job filling me in on everything."

Mayor Dupree laughed. "Well, we're half-brothers, so different last name. My daddy passed and then Mother remarried to Johnny's dad. Joelle, if there's anything I can do while you're staying in Calais, you let me know."

"Thank you," Joelle said. "I will."

The mayor walked across the café to talk to Johnny and took a seat at the counter.

"I guess Johnny got all the brains in the family," Joelle said, "since his brother went for politics."

Alaina laughed. "I'm so glad someone feels the same way about politicians that I do."

"Politicians are the people who keep trying to cut funding at my job so that they can drive fancier cars or have more expensive vacations. It's hard to like people who only think of themselves."

"Isn't that the truth? So getting back to our previous discussion—what did you see?"

Joelle told Alaina about seeing Ophelia's ghost and her theory that she might be too weak to properly communicate.

Alaina slumped back in her seat. "That makes sense as much as anything else about this does. You know, if someone had told me six months ago that I'd be sitting in a café in a tiny bayou town, trying to psychoanalyze a ghost, I'd have called them insane."

"Me, too."

"I wish she'd tell us something concrete."

"Like where her body is?"

Alaina frowned. "That would be a really good place to start. It's all so gruesome, and for a trial attorney to make a comment like that, it's pretty bad."

"This time it's personal."

Alaina gave her a small smile. "You're right. That makes all the difference. So are you going to tell me what else is bothering you?"

"What do you mean?"

"Come on. You have that faraway, slightly disconnected look. I mean, you're in the conversation for the most part, but I can tell that part of you is dwelling on something else. Let me take a stab at it—man problems?"

Joelle sighed. "Am I wearing a sign?"

"It's not so hard to figure out. I've seen Tyler and I've worn that same look before. So what happened?"

Joelle didn't think she'd want to talk about it, not even to her sister, but once she started talking, she poured out everything that had happened the night before and that morning.

Alaina listened without interruption until she finished, then shook her head. "William was certain Tyler was holding in something big—something preventing him from moving forward the way he should be. What a horrible thing to have happen, especially to someone who will feel responsibility even when there was none."

"I know. I wish he'd talk to William, but if it's all the same, I'd prefer if you don't repeat any of this."

"Of course, but I hope Tyler talks to his dad or someone else soon. That's a lot to carry around with you."

"It is, and I understand completely how bad he must feel, but that doesn't mean I will give up my work for him. Not that he's asking me to—he just stormed out and hasn't said a word since."

"I understand how much your work means to you, and I'd be the last person to tell you to change careers. From what I understand from Carter, Tyler isn't the kind of person who would expect it, either. I think he's got a lot of anger and grief he needs to work through, but if he really cares about you, he'll come around."

"If he really cares…" Joelle shook her head. "I was engaged to Brad and he still walked away from me over my work. Maybe I should give up and get a bunch of cats."

"No way am I letting you do that."

"Still holding out hope for a happily ever after?"

"No. I'm allergic."

Joelle laughed. "So am I. Then I guess I'm doomed to a lonely existence free from cat hair."

"Give him some time."

"I guess I don't have a choice. I still have to finish my two weeks, so neither of us is going anywhere." She sighed, the thought of the long day stretching in front of her. "I'm not looking forward to sitting cooped up in that house all day with him. The drive into Calais was incredibly uncomfortable."

"Then I'll come back with you. I mean, once the menfolk allow us back in our house." Alaina grinned.

"I can't ask you to do that."

"You didn't. I'm volunteering. I don't have any client work today and it's high time I got back to helping out around the house. I've got a list of purchased assets from the estate accountant that I've been trying to match to objects in the house, but so far, I've come up empty. I have located quite a few through auction houses, though, so it reinforces our belief that Purcell was selling assets to keep cash coming in."

Joelle felt the tension that had been squeezing her all morning start to melt away. A day working alongside her sister was exactly what she needed to get the ground back underneath her.

"That would be great," she said and smiled.

"Good. Then let's get some breakfast. If Carter and Tyler aren't back by the time we finish, we'll head to my house and work there until we can return to the estate. I've got a whole box of paperwork that I'm going through for Danae."

Joelle nodded as Alaina waved Sonia over to get their order.

She'd have a pleasant breakfast with her sister, then help her sort through estate paperwork. With any luck, the day would be much lower on the excitement scale than the one before.

CARTER LOOKED AT the body lying on the bank of the bayou and compared it to the image on his phone. "Looks like Brant," he said, and showed Tyler his phone with the picture of Brant on it.

Tyler didn't have to take a long look. The man's square jaw and crooked nose in the image were identical to the waterlogged corpse. "At least cause of death isn't a mystery."

The bullet hole in the center of the man's forehead left no doubt as to what had ended Brant's stalking and wife-beating career.

"Yeah," Carter said. "That only leaves the who and the why, but at least it should offer Joelle some comfort."

Tyler nodded. "When I left the Middle East, I never wanted to see another body again, but I have to admit that seeing this one doesn't make me feel anything but relief. Sometimes I wonder what happened to my empathy."

"Hazard of the job." Carter waved at the paramedics who had parked near the dock and were coming down the bank with a gurney.

Tyler watched as they stuffed Brant's body into a black bag and zipped it shut.

One less threat to worry about.

That was true enough, but someone else was still entering the estate, so they weren't in the clear. Then there were his feelings for Joelle.

And that was the biggest threat of all.

Chapter Eighteen

Alaina and Joelle sat at the kitchen table in Carter's cabin and combed through the stack of records they'd taken from Purcell's office. Frustrated by the tedium and lack of pertinent discovery, Joelle tossed a stack of papers on the table and sighed.

"There's nothing here," Joelle said.

Alaina looked as skeptical as she felt, but apparently was not ready to admit defeat. "There's got to be something," she said. "Someone, or more than one someone, is breaking into that house for a reason. Someone besides Brant."

"But you already said you haven't been able to find anything on the asset list the estate accountant sent you. Maybe it's just someone else worried we'll find their name in one of Purcell's payoff notations."

"Maybe, but then why not simply pour gas all over Purcell's office and set it on fire? That's what Roger Martin intended to do." Alaina shook her head. "I've just got this feeling that something else is going on."

"Okay, then let's change tactics. Can I see the asset list? Maybe that will give us a clue."

Alaina pulled a folder out of her briefcase and passed it to Joelle. "The items that I've already tracked to auction houses or art dealers are highlighted in yellow. The rest are unaccounted for."

Joelle flipped through the papers, noting that a good two-thirds of the assets were already highlighted—at least a hundred assets located. "You located this many already?" Her sister's research skills were nothing short of amazing.

"It's not that difficult when you're a fairly well-known attorney and start throwing around words like 'felony theft.'"

Joelle knew Alaina was understating the amount of effort that had gone into tracking down that many of the estate's valuables. She couldn't even imagine the number of phone calls and subtle threats it had taken.

"Some of the things Purcell managed to acquire are amazing," Joelle said as she scanned the list.

"The list of things pre-Purcell is even more impressive. Flip to the end."

Joelle turned to the last page in the folder, her eyes widening at some of the descriptions. "I haven't found any of these things in the house."

"They were probably some of the first to go."

"Seems like it would have been easier for him to just disappear again. I mean, why stay in Calais, closed up in that house, scamming the estate to pay off blackmailers? I don't get it."

Alaina nodded. "I thought the same thing at first. But I think that over time, Purcell started to lose it. I think he stayed for a while thinking he'd make enough money on the sale of estate assets, but once he paid off his helpers, there wasn't much left."

"So he started the buy-and-sell game."

"Exactly, but I think the longer he stayed in the house, the more unstable he became until finally, he was trapped there with his own dark deeds staring him in the face every day."

Joelle looked at the list of assets again. What Alaina said made sense. Purcell thought he had everything planned to collect a fortune and disappear—probably to another country where his mob buddies couldn't find him. He must have grown more desperate with every failed attempt to get out of Calais, and more psychotic with every moment he was forced to remain hidden away in the swamp.

The page she'd turned to only had three missing items on it—a vase, a set of silverware and an entry that simply said "diamonds."

"I guess this was Mother's necklace?" Joelle asked, pointing to the diamonds notation.

"That's what I assumed. It was the only jewelry

listed. Apparently none of the women in our family tree went in for glitter and flash."

"How come it doesn't have an estimated value?"

Alaina shook her head. "I assumed it was because it had never been appraised."

"Probably not. She was so young. Death would have been the last thing on her mind. I guess it's foolish to hope we'll ever find a trace of it."

"My guess is he removed the stones and sold them—melted down the gold."

Bastard. The word echoed through Joelle's mind and she turned her attention back to the paperwork in an attempt to drown it out. She flipped to the next page, then frowned. "A necklace is listed on this page. No other description, but it's got a value of thirty thousand. If the diamond listing was Mother's necklace, then what is this?"

"Let me see." Alaina took the list from her and checked the notations. "I worked on the items so sporadically, I must have missed this. That's some shoddy work."

"You've had a couple of things on your mind besides tracking down stolen property."

Alaina frowned. "I don't remember Mother wearing any other jewelry except the necklace, and that was rare, but then my memory isn't all that reliable. She had a wedding band from her marriage to our father, but I don't think she even had that when she was married to Purcell. I suppose we could call the estate accountant and ask."

"Might as well tie everything down as much as possible," Joelle agreed.

Alaina grabbed her cell phone off the coffee table and dialed the accountant, then put the phone on speaker.

"Leonard, this is Alaina LeBeau," Alaina said when the accountant answered.

"Hello, Ms. LeBeau. What can I do for you today?"

"I'm working on the asset list with my sister Joelle, and we had a question for you."

"I'll be glad to provide any answers that I have."

"Great. On page eight, you have a necklace listed, but on page seventeen, you have a listing that simply reads 'diamonds.' We can't remember our mother owning any valuable jewelry other than her diamond necklace, so we're a bit confused."

"Yes, the necklace listing is for the teardrop diamond necklace I've seen your mother wearing in photographs. I assume that's the one you remember?"

"Yes, that's right. So then what are the diamonds in the other listing, and why don't they have a value assigned?"

"They're a bit of speculation, if you ask me, although the senior partner who has managed your mother's estate for the last forty years assures me they exist, or existed. The story is that your great-grandparents, or some other relative far up the line, acquired some uncut stones reported to be of very high value. The senior partner always assumed that some of them were used to make the necklace your mother wore, as it was a gift from her parents on her eighteenth birthday. But for all we know, the uncut stones never existed, or they used all of them for the necklace and no more remain."

"We've found no record of such stones in the paperwork we've been through so far," Alaina said. "But thank you for the information. If we find anything that seems to confirm the stones' existence, we'll let you know."

"Thank you very much, Ms. LeBeau. I hope you and your sister have a lovely day."

Alaina disconnected the call and looked over at Joelle. "What do you want to bet those stones do exist—or existed?"

"I was thinking the same thing. Uncut diamonds are definitely something Purcell would stick around for, but he must not have found them, or he would have left."

"Maybe Mother wouldn't tell him where they were. Maybe that's why…"

Alaina didn't finish her sentence, but she didn't have to. If Purcell killed Ophelia in a fit of rage over the diamonds, that would explain the cover-up.

"Do you think that's what the others are looking for?" Joelle asked.

Alaina shook her head. "How would they even know about them? Purcell would never have told anyone because he'd want them to himself, and if a rumor about them ever floated through Calais, William or Willamina would have heard it."

"Do you think they existed?"

"Maybe…probably, but maybe it's like the accountant said and they were used to make Mother's necklace."

Joelle sighed. "I suppose that's more logical than thinking a fortune in diamonds has sat undiscovered in the house for decades."

"Another potential lead blasted to shreds. I don't know how Carter does this type of work every day. I thought being a lawyer was hard, but this is simply exhausting."

"It does give me a new appreciation for law enforcement."

"Well, I guess it's back to the paperwork and hopefully a new lead. I have a client meeting tomorrow morning in New Orleans, then I'm going to pay Danae a visit and help her work through some more of the documents. I'll fill her in on the diamond angle so she knows to pay special attention to anything that might mention them."

As Alaina reached for a stack of papers, the front door to the cabin opened and Carter and Tyler walked in. Alaina jumped up from the couch to give Carter a hug. Joelle's heart ached a bit as she watched Alaina wrap her arms around Carter and kiss him gently on the lips.

The look of absolute adoration on Carter's face was so clear, and while Joelle was thrilled for her sister, she couldn't help but want the same thing for herself. Carter was a wonderful man, and he and Alaina were perfect for each other. Before she'd seen them together, Joelle had assumed talk of soul mates was a plot device for romance books, but looking at her sister and Carter, she knew she was wrong. It was possible to have your own happy ending.

She glanced up at Tyler, who stood just inside the doorway. He stared at his friend and Alaina, an odd expression on his face, as though he was trying to make sense of it all. He glanced over at Joelle, but when their eyes met, he immediately looked away. Joelle's chest tightened and another trickle of disappointment ran through her.

"I didn't even hear you pull up," Alaina said when she released Carter.

"Too engrossed in your work," Carter said. "How's it going?"

Alaina filled them in on the diamond theory.

"Doesn't sound like much," Carter said.

"No," Alaina agreed. "We figure it was enough

for Purcell, but we can't think of any way the others would have heard about them."

"They certainly wouldn't have from Purcell."

"That's what we figured. So whoever is breaking into the house is probably looking for something else."

Carter nodded, but Joelle could tell that he wasn't really focusing on the conversation. The tension he'd worn when he first entered the cabin was back, and she wondered if whatever was bothering Carter was part of the reason Tyler seemed even more distant that usual.

"So what were you two doing?" Alaina asked.

She tried to keep the question casual, but Joelle could tell that her sister had sensed something was wrong.

"I got a call this morning that a fisherman found a body washed up on the east bank."

"Oh, no!" Alaina said. "I suppose it's pointless to ask if it's someone you knew, as the town has less than five hundred people. I'm sorry, Carter."

"I'm not. The body was Victor Brant."

Joelle sucked in a breath as the room started to spin. Alaina rushed over to sit beside her and put her arm across her shoulders.

"Breathe deeply," Alaina said.

Joelle let the breath slowly out and some of the dizziness began to subside. Finally, she found her voice. "You're sure it's him?"

Carter nodded. "He hadn't been in the water very long. It was easy to identify him from the photo I passed around. The coroner will do an official identification, of course, but as far as I'm concerned, it's official."

"I can't believe it," Joelle said, her voice barely a whisper.

"It's true," Tyler finally spoke. "I saw him myself and have no doubt it's Brant."

Weeks of tension began to slip from Joelle as she began to realize all the implications Carter's announcement carried. "I'm safe," she said.

"Safe from Brant," Tyler said. "But someone is still entering the house, and given what happened to Alaina and Danae, we're not about to let up on the investigation or the security."

"Tyler's right," Carter agreed. "Don't get me wrong—this is a major improvement for you, Joelle, but we're not about to assume the house is safe. We can't take the risk."

Alaina nodded. "Tyler, if you don't mind, we'd like to do some work at the estate today. We were just waiting on you to return."

"That's fine," Tyler said.

"I can't join you yet," Carter said. "I've got to go talk to the state police and sort everything out with Brant. Joelle, if you know how to get in touch with Brant's wife, now would be the time. The police are going to want to talk to her."

"I will call my point person. They give all the women a prepaid cell phone when they go under. She'll be able to fill her in. Should his wife contact the Jackson police?"

"Yeah. As far as I'm concerned, it's an open-and-shut file. I don't need anything from her. I sent them your statement on Brant's attack yesterday, but they're probably going to want to talk to you in person at some point."

Joelle nodded. That was one conversation she looked forward to having.

It was almost nine o'clock when Joelle, freshly showered, pulled on yoga pants and a T-shirt and propped herself up against the wall in the little twin bed that she and Tyler had shared the night before. Alaina and Carter had stayed late, all four of them working through the house, looking for anything that might provide them a direction for investigation. Alaina and Joelle made spaghetti and garlic bread for dinner and they'd had a pleasant, if not overly dynamic, meal before Alaina and Carter headed home.

Tyler hadn't stood guard outside the bathroom door this time, but she knew he was close by. Now he stuck his head in the bedroom.

"I'm going to shower."

"I don't need to sit in there with you again, do I? I mean, with Brant dead..."

"The immediate danger to you is probably gone. I think you're fine staying in here. You've got your pistol, right?"

She lifted her book from the nightstand, exposing the pistol underneath.

"Good," he said. "Lock the door behind me. I'll knock when I'm done."

He pulled the door closed behind him and Joelle jumped off the bed to push the dead bolt into place. The entire time he'd been talking, Tyler had barely looked at her. She'd hoped with some time passing and Brant's death, that Tyler might loosen his stranglehold on his opinion of her job, as Alaina thought he would. But apparently, he was going to need more time than she'd hoped.

She walked back to the corner and flopped back on the bed. Who was she kidding? Twelve hours wasn't enough time for some people to make up their mind on positioning the toilet paper over versus under, much less change their mind on major life decision points like what kind of woman they wanted to have a relationship with.

What she needed to do was focus on her blessings—and they were many—instead of dwelling on things she couldn't have. Take Brant, for example. Joelle's contact had called her back after relaying the information concerning Brant's death to his wife. The woman had collapsed in tears of joy, and the other rescued women she lived with cheered. That was a victory. It was a shame that they lived in a world that required someone to die in order to let someone else live out their life free of terror, but at least this time, the victim was the one still standing. It had turned out the other way more times than Joelle wanted to remember.

She glanced down at the romance novel lying beside her and sighed. It seemed everywhere she looked a woman was getting a bright future—Alaina, Danae, and always in fiction. When she'd come to Calais, she'd hoped to get her family back, and she had. The money was a huge plus, but not the most important thing, although it was going to allow her to help so many more women than before. What she hadn't expected was to find a man who tugged at her heart the way Tyler did. Somewhere in the midst of all the chaos, she'd tumbled headfirst for the sexy marine, and now, the thought of moving forward without him made her heart ache.

The shower went off in the next room and she grabbed her book, determined to appear collected and aloof. No way would she spend the entire night staring at Tyler like a lovesick puppy. She was going to read her book until she couldn't keep her eyes open any longer, then for the first time since she'd arrived in Calais, she was going to get a good night's sleep.

The knock on the door startled her for a second before she remembered Tyler had her bolt herself in. She jumped up and slid the bolt back, then hurried back to her bed without even a backward glance at Tyler. The bookmark was on page eighty, so that's where she started, but if she was being honest, she couldn't remember a thing about the story. Still, she was determined to look busy, so she focused on the words and started to read.

It lasted about two seconds.

Tyler stood with his back to her, his hair still damp from the shower. He had on sweatpants but no shirt, and one look at his marvelously cut back had her hands itching to touch every inch of him as she had the night before. He bent over to retrieve a T-shirt out of his suitcase, and she held in a sigh.

It was going to be a very, very long night.

He pulled the T-shirt over his head, then sat on his bed with his back against the wall, clutching a file folder. Joelle had heard him request some police records from Carter, and the stamp on the outside was a dead giveaway. Apparently, Tyler intended to do some night reading, as well.

Fine.

She pulled the pillow behind her back to a more comfortable position, then dove back into her book. Before she knew it, her eyes were drooping—the events of the day finally catching up with her— and she dropped off to sleep.

SHE WASN'T SUPPOSED to be out of bed, but Joelle loved the still night air of the house—loved roaming around its vast open areas and dozens of nooks and crannies when no one else stirred. Things were reversed, she thought. If she could stay up all night and sleep all morning, life would be perfect.

Well, as perfect as it could be with him in the house.

She'd begged Mommy the night before, and that was something Joelle never did. Begging was for little girls with no manners, but she'd abandoned all training and begged Mommy to make the bad man leave. Mommy had hugged her and cried and whispered that she wanted to make him leave, but she couldn't just yet. She'd asked Joelle to be patient like the big girl Mommy knew she was.

Tonight, Joelle had crept into the attic. In all the ancient trunks, the attic held untold treasures—dresses and shoes from so long ago, you could only see them in books. Joelle loved trying on the beautiful layers of satin and lace and standing in front of the dusty mirror to try to figure out what she'd look like when she was older. She hoped she looked like Mommy, as Mommy was the most beautiful lady in the world. Alaina already looked like Mommy and it made Joelle jealous of her older sister.

She had no idea what time it was when she crept out of the attic staircase and onto the second-floor landing, but it had been dark outside for some time.

She paused at the edge of the hallway and peeked around at the balcony. All she had to do was scurry down one side of the balcony and she'd be at the hallway to the bedroom. Then she was in the clear.

The balcony was empty and silent, so she slipped around the corner and hurried down the carpeted runner in the center of the wooden flooring. But when she was halfway to the safety zone, she heard the front door open and hushed voices echoed up from the entry. Immediately, she dropped on her hands and knees so that they couldn't see her if they looked upstairs. She recognized one of the voices as the bad man. The other voice was low and raspy.

She waited, hoping they'd move off to the kitchen or one of the formal areas on the first floor, because if they came upstairs, she was caught for sure. No way could she make it across the balcony, down the hall and into her bedroom before they climbed the stairs. Praying that the wooden floors didn't squeak, she started to crawl toward the hallway, staying as far away from the balcony as the carpeted runner allowed.

She'd only made it a couple of feet before she heard Mommy. The fear in Mommy's voice made her freeze again. Joelle knew Mommy was afraid of the bad man, but she'd never heard her sound like this. Something was wrong—even more wrong than usual.

She crept to the edge of the balcony and lay down

flat, peering over the edge. Mommy was standing next to the bad man near the front door. All she could see of the raspy man was his legs as the rest of him was hidden by the staircase.

"You'll tell me or you'll pay," the bad man said.

"I don't know," Mommy cried, her voice shaking.

"Lying bitch," the bad man said and struck Mommy with his hand, knocking her to the floor. "Grab her!"

Joelle saw hands reach from behind the staircase and clutch Mommy's shoulders, preventing her from rising—preventing her from escaping. The bad man pulled something from his pocket and poked Mommy in the arm with it. She struggled, but couldn't get away. Then she went completely limp and her eyes rolled back in her head.

Joelle began to scream and everything went black.

"JOELLE, WAKE UP!" The voice sounded above her and she bolted upright, then clutched her head as a wave of nausea ran through her.

"Can you hear me?" Tyler's voice registered somewhere in her frantic mind, and she looked up at him and nodded.

He dropped onto the bed next to her and gathered her in his arms. She clutched him, her heart pounding so strongly in her chest she swore she could hear it echo in the dead silence of the room.

Her mind spun with what she'd seen—what she'd remembered.

Tyler pushed back from her and studied her face. "Are you all right? You started screaming and I couldn't wake you."

"I remembered something—something horrible."

"What?"

She sucked in a breath, her heart pounding in her temples and making her head swim.

"I saw Purcell kill our mother."

Chapter Nineteen

Tyler placed a cup of coffee in front of Joelle along with cream and sugar, then he took a seat next to her at the breakfast table. It was only 5:00 a.m. when Joelle had startled him out of bed, but one look at her wide eyes and pale skin and Tyler knew she wouldn't be able to sleep again anytime soon. Her terror-filled screams had sent him hurtling back to a past he'd been trying to lock away, and his pulse still beat stronger even twenty minutes after he'd sprung up from his bed, certain someone was killing her.

After her statement, she'd collapsed in tears, then after gaining a bit of composure, locked herself in the bathroom for a bit. When she'd finally emerged, Tyler suggested they head downstairs for coffee and to talk. With all the overhead lights on, the kitchen would be bright and cheery, and Tyler wanted her to wind down enough to tell him what she'd remembered.

Her hands shook as she added sugar to her coffee

and Tyler's guilt over adding a shot of whiskey to it melted away. His anxiety grew with every second she continued to stir, staring blankly into the cup, but finally, she pulled the spoon out and lifted the cup to her lips.

When she took the first sip, her eyes widened and she looked at him.

"Whiskey," he said.

She nodded and took another long sip, then she lowered the cup and frowned.

"I can get you something else," he said.

"No. That's not it." Her brow creased and she took another sip, then stared at him. "The milk."

He jumped up from his chair. "I'll get the milk."

"No!" she said.

He sat back down, completely confused.

"I'm sorry," she said. "I don't want milk. I remembered something about milk. Every night before bed, Purcell made us a glass of warm milk. He claimed it made you sleep better, but I never liked it. It always tasted bitter to me—like the coffee did."

"You think Purcell doctored your milk?"

"It would make sense, right? He usually left the room long enough for me to dump it out, but Alaina always drank it. When I started remembering things that happened when I was roaming the house at night, I wondered why none of the fights woke Alaina up, but whiskey would explain that, right?"

Tyler clenched his jaw at the thought of Purcell drugging his stepdaughters so that he could abuse their mother. Truly, there was no end to the evil he'd brought into their lives. "It may also explain why her memory is so foggy despite her being the oldest."

Joelle's eyes widened. "You're right." She shook her head. "For a bodyguard, it seems you've spent a lot of time helping me work through my childhood issues."

"It's all part of the same service," he said and gave her an encouraging smile.

"Well, the service has been exemplary. And you've been very patient, fixing me coffee and coddling me, but it's time I tell you what I saw."

"Were you dreaming?"

"Yes, but I'm certain that what I saw really happened." She paused for a second and stared out the window into the darkness, then looked back at him. "I didn't tell you everything about the last time I remembered something from my childhood."

"I had a feeling that was the case, but I think you need to tell me everything now."

She nodded. "That night in the hallway wasn't the first time I remembered what I told you about—the argument between my mother and Purcell. I've carried that with me for as long as I can remember, but being here and recalling it made it feel so much worse."

He nodded. It made sense that being back in the house would make everything seem more vivid.

"He hit her," Joelle blurted out, almost as if she had to get it out before she changed her mind. "I saw him hit her so hard she fell and then just stayed there, huddled up and crying while he stood over her and screamed."

Tyler's jaw involuntarily clenched and anger coursed through him as he processed her witnessing her mother's abuse so young. "I'm sorry. No one should ever have to see such things."

"That's the reason why…"

"Why, what?"

She looked directly at him, her eyes filled with tears. "Why I do the work I do. I couldn't help my mother, but if I can prevent another child from living that nightmare, then I have to do it."

A rush of regret ran through Tyler as he remembered his harsh words to Joelle about her profession. Her choice of profession was so personal, and he'd used her doing the right thing as a reason to prevent her from entering his life. Shame followed the regret, and he tried to push it down. For all those medals he had locked away in a box, he was a coward.

"I can't quit," she said. "Even if I wanted to, my conscience wouldn't let me."

He put his hand over hers. "I shouldn't have assumed you would. What you're doing is important. I was selfish to think you'd give it up simply because I was too afraid to deal with my own issues."

The relief on her face was so clear that a second wave of guilt washed over him. He'd let his own inability to deal with his past allow him to try to force someone else into a neat little box just so he could feel better about caring for them.

He gave her hand a squeeze. "What did you see in your dream?"

She took another drink of coffee, then began to talk. He listened intently—his pulse increasing with every word—as she described in horrifying detail what she'd seen looking down from the banister.

When she finished, he blew out a breath. "You didn't see the other man?"

"No. I just heard his voice."

"Raspy…could it have been Amos?" As soon as the words left his mouth, he hated saying them, but now was not the time for sentimental thoughts. Every angle must be explored.

Her eyes widened. "No! No way."

"You're one hundred percent positive that it couldn't have been him?"

"Of course…well, I'm sure…." She clasped her hands over her mouth. "Oh, no. I can't be positive, but surely it couldn't be. Amos loved us girls and our mother."

Tyler nodded. "That's what we've all thought, but he's been in the perfect position to know everything that goes on in this house, including knowing about any valuables that Purcell acquired."

"But his foot is broken," Joelle argued, refusing to buy into Amos being a bad guy. "He couldn't have been out on my balcony or strolling in front of your cameras."

Tyler frowned. "No, none of those could have been him, but he could be working with someone else."

"I hate this! Suspecting people who claim they care about you."

She was so distressed that he rose and pulled her up from her chair to hold her. They stood there, arms wrapped around each other for a while, and when he finally released her, he placed his hands on both sides of her face and lowered his lips to hers. She responded with such passion, and his heart swelled with emotion.

"Are you sure about this? About us?" she whispered when they finished the kiss.

"It may be the only thing I'm sure about."

She broke into a smile so beautiful it made him feel warm all over. He wasn't about to fool himself into thinking it would be easy. A lot of unresolved issues lay in the back of his mind, just waiting to resurface at the most inconvenient times. If he wanted to move forward, he was going to have to face them all.

But for the first time in years, he thought it might be possible.

ALAINA TOSSED A stack of paper in the recycle box and stretched before flopping back onto the recliner. She and Danae had been sitting in Zach's living room, sorting through LeBeau estate paperwork for three hours. They still hadn't unearthed anything that gave them a clue as to who else Purcell was involved with or what exactly had happened to their mother, and not even a hint of information on the elusive diamonds.

"How's Zach?" Alaina asked. She'd been waiting for Danae to offer the information, but either her sister was dense or being protective. Alaina didn't believe Danae was capable of being dense, so the second option was the most likely.

Danae glanced over at her, then back down at the coffee table. "He says he's all right."

"But you don't believe him?"

Danae shook her head. "He's better than before but the guilt is eating him up. Every day that passes and we don't know what happened to Mother's body, it's like adding five pounds to the weight he's already carrying."

"He's not responsible for what his father did. None of us think that."

Danae gave her a grateful smile. "I know, and deep down, so does he. But I'm afraid of what will happen if we never find the answers. I'm afraid of what he'll become if he lives his whole life under this shadow."

"Oh, baby sister." Alaina rose from her chair and sat next to Danae on the couch to give her a hug. "We're not going to let that happen."

Alaina released her and grabbed a stack of paper. "I have a good feeling about this stack." She divided the stack in half and held half out to Danae.

Danae laughed and grabbed the papers. "You've said that about every stack for the last three hours."

"Those were practice runs."

"Eternal optimist."

"Nope," Alaina said as she scanned the first page. "Desperate realist."

Danae laughed and started reviewing the papers. Alaina scanned the first sheet for large dollar amounts, then finding none, flipped it over and started on the next sheet. She trailed her finger down the yellowed paper, expecting that this was another page of house supplies and gas bills and suddenly she froze.

An entry for twenty thousand dollars—the same amount Purcell had used to pay off others.

She looked to the left, hoping the entry was legible. Her heart leaped in her throat when she saw a single last name.

Picard.

"I found something," Alaina said, her voice cracking. "Look."

Danae leaned over to view the paper. "It's the same twenty thousand," she said, the excitement clear in her voice. "Do you know anyone in Calais with the name Picard?"

Alaina slowly shook her head. "I'm mentally running through everyone, but I don't think I've ever heard of someone by that name in Calais. How about you?"

"It doesn't ring a bell, and I'm sure I met everyone when I worked at the café."

"But it sounds familiar." Suddenly, Alaina bolted off the couch. "I got it!"

Danae jumped up beside her. "Who?"

"The family doctor. Doc Broussard said our mom took us all to her doctor in New Orleans—the doctor her parents had always used. I'm almost positive Doc Broussard said his name was Picard."

Danae flopped back down on the couch and grabbed her laptop. She tapped in a search, and Alaina leaned over to see the screen.

"There's a Dr. Richard Picard in New Orleans,"

Danae said and clicked on a link. "But it looks like he's retired."

"That would be reasonable. If he was our grandparents' doctor, he can't be young. What about a home address?"

Danae tapped again and came up with an address in a wealthy historic district. "No telephone number. Do you think Carter's friends at the New Orleans Police Department would be willing to get it for him?"

"Probably, but I don't know that it's a good idea to call. You can't see someone's expression over the phone, and even scheduling an appointment would let them know you're coming."

"So you're thinking just show up and have Carter flash a badge?"

Alaina smiled. "It *is* really handy sleeping with a cop."

A knock on the condo door interrupted them and Alaina went to open it.

"Speak of the devil," she said as she gave Carter a kiss.

"What did I do now?" he asked.

"Nothing yet," Alaina said as Danae jumped up from the couch to give him a quick hug. "It's what you're going to do."

He narrowed his eyes at them. "You found something."

"Oh, yeah," Alaina said and she and Danae showed him their work.

"So what are we waiting for?" Carter asked. "Let's pay him a visit."

Alaina jumped up and down and clapped her hands. Danae checked her watch and groaned. "I have class in half an hour, and we're having a test. Go, then come back and tell me everything!"

"Of course," Alaina said and grabbed her purse.

Fifteen minutes later, Carter steered his truck up a huge circular drive and parked in front of a plantation-style house with white columns and blue shutters. They walked to the front door, and Alaina bit her lower lip as Carter rang the doorbell.

Within seconds, an older lady wearing light blue scrubs opened the door. "Can I help you?"

Carter showed her his badge and her eyebrows went up.

"I'm Sheriff Carter Trahan from Calais and this is Alaina LeBeau. I'm conducting an investigation and need to ask some questions."

"The police? I can't imagine what anyone in this household would have to do with the police."

"It's an old matter," Carter said, "and one that I'd like to put to rest. Can we speak to Dr. Picard?"

"I'm sorry," the woman said. "You're about five years too late for that."

Alaina's hopes fell. "Perhaps Mrs. Picard could help us. Do you care for her?"

The nurse nodded. "I'm sorry to disappoint you, but Mrs. Picard can't even help herself. She's in the late stages of Alzheimer's. Most days, she thinks she's back in grade school. By the time he passed, she'd already forgotten the doctor, and they'd been married over forty years."

"Oh, that's so sad," Alaina said.

"Yes, ma'am, it is. I wish I could help."

"Thank you for your time," Carter said and he put his arm around Alaina as they walked away.

"Wait!" The nurse hurried down the sidewalk after them and grabbed Alaina's arm. "Did you say your name was LeBeau?"

"Yes. Alaina LeBeau. My mother, Ophelia, was a patient of the doctor's."

"All these years... I never thought..." she said, her eyes wide. "I better explain. Dr. Picard died of pulmonary disease, but it took a while to happen. Toward the end, he gave me an envelope and said if anyone by the name of LeBeau came looking for him, I was to give them the envelope."

Alaina sucked in a breath. "And you still have it?"

The nurse nodded. "I stuck it in the desk drawer and forgot all about it. I figured it was the ravings of a dying man. I never actually thought someone would come. Let me go get it."

She hurried back inside and Alaina clutched Carter's arm, unable to control her excitement. "Maybe he felt guilty like Zach's dad. The letter might explain everything."

"Let's not get our hopes up just yet," Carter warned, but Alaina could tell he was as excited by the potential as she was.

It seemed like forever, but was probably only minutes before the nurse hurried back out with the envelope. She handed it to Alaina and smiled. "I hope it has the answers you're looking for."

Alaina clutched the envelope as the nurse walked back into the house and shut the door. She looked up at Carter. "I'm afraid to open it. What if it doesn't say anything? What if he was out of his mind and he stuffed his grocery list in here?"

"Then we'll keep going," he said. "I'm not going to quit until we have answers to all of your questions. Every single one."

She smiled at him, her heart swelling with love and pride for the man she was going to marry. She'd never even known a man like him existed, much less that she'd find him and he'd want to be with her.

Her hands shook as she tore the corner off the envelope and slipped her finger inside to tear it open. For a second, she worried that it might be empty and all of this buildup would have been for nothing, but a single sheet of paper lay inside.

She pulled it out and unfolded it, her heart pounding as she looked at the shaky cursive, then she began to read it out loud.

To whoever comes for this letter,
Twenty years ago, I did a horrible thing. The reason why I did it is unimportant and doesn't excuse my actions, so I won't go into it.

I helped Trenton Purcell get rid of his wife, Ophelia LeBeau.

I have regretted it every day since I deposited the money, but by then it was too late. If I'd confessed, I would have been stripped of my medical license and my wife and kids would have lost everything. I couldn't make them suffer for my bad decision, so I said nothing.

But it's eaten away at me like a cancer.

I knew he was going to send her to Eleanor, but I didn't think he would leave her there. I'm sorry for what happened to her children and to her. If I could go back and change things, I would. Every day, I ask God to forgive me, and every day, I am worried that he can't.

My sin was too great.
Richard Picard

Alaina clutched the letter and read it again silently. Finally, she looked up at Carter, more confused than ever. "He didn't say he helped Purcell kill her. He says they sent her to Eleanor...but who is Eleanor?"

"You haven't run across that name in any of the documents you've helped Danae catalog?"

She shook her head. "I don't know anyone named Eleanor."

"Maybe the nurse knows."

They hurried back to the front door and rang the bell again. The nurse seemed surprised to see them again.

"Is everything all right?" she asked.

"In the letter that Dr. Picard left," Alaina said, "he said he sent my mother to Eleanor. Do you have any idea who that is?"

"Eleanor isn't a person, dear. It's a sanitarium."

Thoughts of tuberculosis raced through Alaina's mind. "What was wrong with her?"

The nurse gave Alaina a sympathetic look. "Eleanor Roosevelt Sanitarium cares for the mentally ill."

"Oh!" Alaina's hand flew over her mouth.

"Thank you, again," Carter said as he placed his arm around Alaina's shoulders and led her back to the truck.

"He had her committed and then told everyone she'd died," Alaina said as she stared out the windshield. "That's why there was no body in the casket. That's what he paid them to cover up."

Carter pulled out his cell phone and called information to get the number for the sanitarium. He put the phone on speaker as it dialed.

"Thank you for calling Eleanor Roosevelt Mental Treatment Facility. Can I help you?" the receptionist asked.

"Yes, I'd like to inquire about a patient you had there twenty-five years ago."

"Mrs. Anderson has been in charge of medical records for over thirty years. If anyone can help you, it will be her."

"Great. Can I speak to her?"

"She's on vacation and doesn't return until the day after tomorrow, but I can make you an appointment for then. Is ten o'clock okay?"

"That's great. My name is Carter Trahan, and I'll have some family members with me."

"Okay, Mr. Trahan, I have you down for ten o'clock."

"Thank you." Carter disconnected the call. "Looks like we have to wait a couple of days."

"I know. At first, I wanted to scream, but this way is better. This way, Danae and Joelle can go with us. Just in case…."

Carter reached over and squeezed her hand. "Just in case."

ALAINA COULD HARDLY contain herself as she rushed to the front door of the estate and fumbled with her key.

"Don't open it," Carter yelled from behind her. "The alarm is probably set."

"Oh, I forgot." She slipped the key back in her purse and banged on the door, hoping Tyler and Joelle were somewhere they could easily hear. A couple seconds later, the door opened a crack and Tyler peered out, then he stepped back and they hurried inside.

"We have news," Alaina said. "Where's Joelle?"

"She's in the kitchen. We were just about to fix some sandwiches. Are you interested?"

"That would be great," Carter said. "We didn't stop on the way back from New Orleans. Alaina was in too big a hurry to get here."

Tyler raised his eyebrows. "This must be good."

"Oh, yeah," Alaina said as she hurried down the hallway, silently willing the two men to get the lead out.

Joelle stood at the counter, putting lettuce on turkey sandwiches. She looked up and smiled when she saw Alaina. "I thought I heard your voice," Joelle said.

Tyler and Carter stepped into the kitchen behind her and Alaina grabbed Joelle's hands, unable to hold her news in any longer.

"We found something," Alaina said, then explained what she and Danae discovered and her and Carter's visit to the doctor. She pulled the letter out of her purse and handed it to Joelle. Tyler stepped behind Joelle and read over her shoulder.

"Wow!" Joelle said. "This makes so much sense now."

"It does?" Alaina looked surprised.

Joelle nodded and told them about her dream. "So the needle wasn't used to kill her. They sedated her."

"That fits with everything," Carter said, "but I'd still like to know how Purcell got her committed. You can't just drop someone off at a mental institution and claim they're sick when they're not."

"I think she was cracking," Joelle said. "The stress and abuse could have put her over the edge. And there's something else…something that I can't prove, but I believe happened."

Joelle told them about her suspicion that Purcell had spiked their milk each night.

"You were always able to stay up later than me," Alaina said. "I could barely get in bed before I was out."

"Exactly," Joelle said. "So if he was doing it to us, why wouldn't he have done it to Mother?"

"As despicable as it sounds," Alaina said, "I've seen it before in child custody cases where one parent wants to make the other look incompetent. If Purcell drugged our mother to the point that she seemed incoherent and erratic, all he'd need was a doctor's assessment and a couple of credible witnesses to say she was behaving irrationally. He paid for the doctor's assessment—he could have paid for witnesses. If he made a case for child endangerment, it would have been enough to commit her."

"But why?" Joelle said. "Why keep her alive?"

Alaina shook her head. "It sounds like he wanted something and Mother wouldn't tell him what he wanted to know."

"The diamonds?" Joelle said.

"It's possible. Maybe Purcell thought there was more than just her necklace, and he didn't believe her when she said she didn't know. He might have figured that locking her up would make her tell."

Joelle stared at Alaina, her eyes wide. "Then what happened to her after that? I mean she died at some point or she wouldn't be haunting us, but I always assumed she died here since she appears here."

"Maybe he brought her back here at some point and killed her then."

"That could be. Did you tell Danae and Zach?"

Alaina nodded. "We went by Zach's place before heading back to Calais. We wanted to tell him in person that it didn't look like his father was involved in a murder. He's still not happy about his father's decision to bury an empty casket, but I think he's relieved that it's a lesser sin than what he feared."

Alaina looked out the kitchen window, all the day's events running through her mind. For the first time since she'd arrived in Calais, she finally felt that they were on the right track—that they were finally going to get the answers about everything that happened so long ago.

Suddenly, she froze. "There's something out there."

"Where?" Carter asked, shifting immediately into cop mode.

"In the brush about twenty feet from the house. It was big and moved quickly."

"Bear?" Tyler asked.

"Unless it was walking on hind legs and thinner than the average bear, no."

Carter pulled his pistol from his waistband. "Let's check it out," he said to Tyler, then turned to Joelle and Alaina. "Keep the doors locked and your weapons ready."

The two men rushed outside and Alaina locked the door behind them, already worried about what lurked in the swamp. "Do you have your pistol?" she asked Joelle.

"It's upstairs on the nightstand."

Alaina pulled her pistol from her purse. "Run up and get it. I'll wait in the entry where I can see the balcony."

Alaina followed Joelle to the entry and watched as she hurried up the stairs and into one of the bedrooms. By the time she heard the footsteps behind her, it was too late.

A cloth covered her mouth and nose, a hand pressed against it and an arm wrapped around her back. She struggled for a second, then everything went black.

Chapter Twenty

Relief coursed through Joelle when she saw her pistol on the nightstand where she'd left it that morning. She grabbed it and rushed out of the room.

"Got it!" she yelled down at Alaina.

Her own voice echoed back at her and she drew up short and peered over the balcony. Her heart caught in her throat as she scanned the entry. Alaina was nowhere in sight.

"Alaina!" she called down.

Nothing.

Maybe something happened outside. Maybe Alaina went to help Carter and Tyler.

Clutching her pistol, she inched toward the staircase, scanning below her with every step. There was no sign of Alaina anywhere and no sound echoed up from the entry. She leaned over the railing, trying to look down the kitchen hallway.

When she rose back up, she felt cold metal press against her scalp.

"Drop it," he said.

She let her pistol slide out of her hand and onto the carpeted runner. His voice sounded familiar, but she couldn't place it.

"Now," he said and coughed. "Turn around. Slowly."

Terror coursed through her as the raspy voice from her nightmare rang through her head. It was him. The man who'd helped Purcell attack her mother. The man who'd held her mother down while Purcell drugged her.

Her feet seemed to move involuntarily. She didn't want to turn, but she couldn't keep herself from doing it. She clenched her eyes shut until the gun pressed directly into the center of her forehead, then opened them and stared at the man who'd helped ruin her childhood.

Mayor Dupree!

"I don't understand," she said. "Why would you help Purcell?"

He lowered his pistol and took a step back from her. "The oldest reason in the world—money."

"Fine. That was twenty-five years ago. You got away with it. Why bother with me now and risk exposing yourself?"

His eyes narrowed at her. "Because when you talked to me in the café with your sister, you recognized me. It was only a matter of time before you remembered why."

"I never saw you that night. I only heard you."

He sighed. "Then I guess this is going to be a waste of a bullet."

As he lifted the pistol up toward her head, she screamed.

TYLER AND CARTER hurried through the swamp to the spot Alaina had indicated. Two clear footprints stared up at them from the soft ground.

"This way," Tyler said and headed through the swamp in the direction the steps pointed. As he ran through a thick set of brush, his feet connected with something heavy and large and he grabbed hold of a tree trunk to keep from falling.

Carter slid to a stop behind him and they looked down at the crumpled body of Bert Thibodeaux.

Tyler immediately dropped down and put his fingers to Bert's neck. "He's alive."

Carter stooped and helped Tyler roll Bert over onto his back, then Tyler tapped his cheeks. "Bert. Wake up."

The burly truck driver stirred a bit, then bolted upright.

"Oh, my head," Bert said and clutched his head with both hands.

"What happened?" Tyler said.

"What does it look like? Someone cracked me on the head."

"Did you see who did it?"

"No. He came up behind me."

"You're in a lot of trouble, Bert," Carter said. "A lot of things have gone wrong in this house and I can put you on the hook for all of them if I want."

Bert's eyes widened and for the first time, Tyler saw a glimmer of fear in them. "I haven't hurt nobody. That ain't my thing."

"Then maybe it's time you tell me exactly what your thing is. Or I can haul you in now."

Bert studied Carter's face for a while, and Tyler wondered if the stubborn trucker was about to clam up again, but apparently he figured out that Carter wasn't joking about pinning everything on him.

Finally, he sighed. "I was looking for the diamonds."

Carter's eyes narrowed on him. "How did you know about the diamonds? And don't tell me Purcell told you, because I'm sure he took that secret to the grave hoping to find them himself."

Bert looked down at the ground. "Roger Martin told me. I don't know how he found out."

He was lying. Tyler would bet anything on it, and one look at Carter's face told him his friend didn't buy it either. But what was Bert hiding now?

Or who?

It hit Tyler like a shock wave—the red lacy bra suddenly stringing everything together.

"Sonia," Tyler said. "It was Sonia who told you."

Bert's eyes widened and Tyler knew he was right.

"Johnny said she dated a numbers guy. What do

you want to bet it was the estate accountant," Tyler said. "She did it for the information and always intended to come back here to you."

One look at Bert's face and Tyler knew his guess was correct.

Carter whistled. "That's one even I didn't see coming. How have you been getting in the house?"

Defeated, Bert inclined his head toward a set of brush to their right. "Same as always. Through the tunnel."

Tyler stared at Bert for a moment as he remembered the footprints near the house but not leading up to it and the small clearing he'd discovered that first day. The clearing they were standing in now. "The cellar. It connects to the cellar in the butler's pantry."

Tyler pulled the brush and a huge tangle of dead vines came away, exposing a wooden door. "Brant must have seen someone use it. That's how he got in before."

Carter nodded. "And that same someone put a bullet in him before he could make matters worse. And likely cracked our friend Bert here on the head."

"Well," Bert said, "whoever it was is in the house now. The door was still covered with dirt when I got here."

"Get out of here and have your head looked at," Carter told Bert. "I'll be by later to take your statement. Don't even think of leaving town or you'll have more trouble than you'll ever work your way out of."

Bert knew when he was defeated. He gave Carter a single nod and hoisted himself up from the ground. They watched as he stumbled through the brush back toward the house, still clutching his head.

Tyler pulled back the wooden door and peered inside.

"It's not deep," he said and climbed down the ladder into the pit. Carter pulled a penlight out of his pocket and dropped it to him.

"I'm going to circle around and enter through the front door so maybe we can corner this bastard once and for all. Be careful when you get to the cellar. He could be in there waiting for you."

Tyler gave him a nod and directed the penlight down the tunnel. The tunnel was so narrow only one person could fit through it at a time, and he had to duck a bit to keep from scraping his head on the ceiling. The entire thing was composed of chopped stone, and Tyler wondered briefly how long the tunnel had been there. The craftsmanship of the stonework led him to believe it was very old.

He hurried down it, careful not to bang his head against the ceiling. It shouldn't take long to reach the cellar entrance given the proximity of the trapdoor from the house. As he rounded a corner, he drew up short. A door made of thick wooden planks and steel belts was directly in front of him.

He pressed his ear against it, but couldn't hear anything. That didn't mean the room was clear, though. Gripping the penlight with his left hand and pistol with his right, he pressed his shoulder against the door and eased it open enough to peer inside. He cast his penlight across the cellar, but didn't see anyone.

Relieved, he stepped out of the tunnel and into the cellar, then turned back to look as the door swung shut. The cellar side was finished with a sheet of paneling that blended perfectly with the rest of the wall, explaining why he hadn't noticed it before. He shone the penlight around the edges of the paneling, now able to make out the outline of the door.

Clever.

He headed up the cellar stairs, wondering if Carter had made it inside the house yet. When he reached the door to the butler's pantry, he paused again, to listen for footsteps. Hearing nothing, he eased the door open a crack and that's when a bloodcurdling scream echoed throughout the house.

Joelle!

He bolted out of the cellar and tore through the kitchen in the direction of the scream, almost tripping over Alaina's prone body in the hallway. He paused only long enough to ensure she was breathing then took off again. What if he was too late? What if, once again, he failed?

Although he didn't think it possible, he ramped his speed up another notch, not about to repeat the worst moment of his life. Especially not now, when it was more important that he succeed than any other time.

Because he couldn't imagine his life without Joelle in it.

He ran into the massive entry, pistol raised and scanning the area for any sign of Joelle. Voices sounded above him and he ran out from under the overhang. What he saw made his blood run cold. A man had Joelle's neck clutched in one hand and his pistol in the other, and even though his back was to Tyler, he recognized the frame he'd seen leaving the general store a couple of days before.

Joelle's face turned red as she pulled at his arm with both hands, unable to break free from his grasp. Her eyes rolled back in her head and Tyler had to force himself from running upstairs and beating the man to death with his bare hands.

Think smart, Duhon!

Lifting his pistol, Tyler tried to get a clear shot, but Dupree was too close to her. If he took a shot, the bullet might go through Dupree and into Joelle.

She gasped for air and her eyes flickered down and she caught sight of Tyler. He pointed down with his finger, hoping she'd understand what he wanted her to do. Dupree lifted the pistol, his finger positioned on the trigger, and Tyler sighted his gun on the back of the man's head, praying that Joelle acted quickly—before it was too late.

Suddenly, her legs buckled and she dropped to the ground. Without even thinking, Tyler took the shot, and it was deadly accurate.

The bullet passed straight through Dupree's head and hit the paneling on the wall in front of him, splintering the wood as it entered. At the same time, the front door flew open and the alarm went off as Carter ran inside.

Tyler ran up the stairs two at a time and rushed over to Joelle, who was crumpled on the floor. He glanced at Dupree as he passed, but it was clear the man was no longer a threat. He reached down to touch Joelle's face, worried that the strain had caused her to pass out or even worse, go into cardiac arrest, but as his fingers touched her cheek, she opened her eyes and smiled before leaping up into his arms.

Downstairs, Tyler heard Carter call for an ambulance as he clutched Joelle close to him, saying a silent prayer of thanks that the woman who'd changed his life was still here with him. And if he had his way, she was going to be part of his life every day from this point forward.

"I thought I'd lost you," he whispered. "I couldn't have taken it."

"I know," Joelle said. "After what you'd been through before, I can't imagine how you felt, thinking you might not be able to save me."

"It wasn't failure that scared me." He pulled back a bit and looked down at her. "It was the thought of losing you. I don't pretend to have all the answers, or that us being involved will be without issues, but now that I've met you, I can't imagine my life without you."

Her eyes widened. "Are you sure?"

"It's the only thing in my life I *am* sure about."

She smiled and threw her arms around him again. He stroked her hair and felt her heart beating strong against his chest, and knew without a single doubt that he never wanted to let her go.

"How did you get inside?" she asked.

Tyler told her about the tunnel and finding Bert, who had been trying to find the diamonds.

Her eyes widened and she sucked in a breath. "I know where they are."

"What?"

"The diamonds." Joelle smiled, then started laughing. "They've been here all along."

"Where?"

"In a purple Crown Royal bag tucked underneath the seat of a school desk. They look like rocks—just like the rocks in the driveway."

"Then how do you know…"

"Because Mother gave them to me and told me

never to let Purcell see them. I'd bet everything I'll inherit that those diamonds have been tucked under the seat of that desk for over twenty-five years."

Tyler smiled, trying to wrap his mind around what Joelle said. "Wouldn't that be perfect?"

Joelle's smile faded. "It's not perfect until we find our mother, but it's going to happen. We're going to find out what happened to our mother and I'm going to move to Calais and start a life with you."

He gathered her in his arms again. "Sounds perfect to me," he whispered.

Chapter Twenty-One

Two days later

Joelle stopped at the entrance to the Eleanor Roosevelt Mental Treatment Facility and looked at Alaina and Danae. "Are you ready?" she asked.

They looked at each other, then back at her and nodded. Carter, Zach and Tyler stood behind them, a unified front supporting them. Tyler gave her a thumbs-up and she smiled.

"Let's do this, then," she said and pulled open the door.

Joelle walked up to the receptionist desk with Alaina and Danae. "Hi," she said. "We have an appointment with Mrs. Anderson. Well, the appointment is for Carter Trahan."

The receptionist checked her log and smiled. "Please step through the secured door when the buzzer sounds and I'll have Marie escort you to Mrs. Anderson's office."

The buzzer seemed incredibly loud in the relative

quiet of the building, but Joelle pulled open the door and they all stepped through, where Marie greeted them and led them down several long, white hallways and into a room at the end of the hall.

A large woman with a big head of white hair met them at the front of an enormous room. Shelves, standing a good eight feet tall, ran in long rows from the front of the room to the back. File folders filled every shelf, and Joelle felt a wave of sadness run through her that so many people had needed such a place.

"Carter Trahan?" the woman asked.

Carter stepped forward and extended his hand. "I'm Carter. You must be Mrs. Anderson."

She smiled. "Please call me Emily. You weren't lying about bringing family with you, were you?"

"No, ma'am," he said and introduced everyone. "These three ladies think their mother might have been a patient here twenty-five years ago."

Emily frowned. "Then why don't you ask her?"

Carter explained briefly about Ophelia's supposed death and the dispersal of the sisters.

Emily's eye grew wider and wider and when Carter finished, she shook her head, giving the sisters a sympathetic look. "What a horrible story. I sure hope I can get you some answers. Grab some of those chairs and drag them over to my desk."

Three chairs were positioned against the wall. The men dragged them over in front of Emily's desk and Alaina, Danae and Joelle each took a seat as the men circled around the side of the desk.

"What was your mother's name?" Emily asked.

"Ophelia LeBeau," Alaina said.

Emily tapped on the computer, then scrolled through records, shaking her head. "No one by the name of LeBeau has ever been admitted here."

Joelle's heart dropped. Surely they hadn't come all this way for nothing. "Are you certain?"

Emily nodded. "I've been entering the historical records myself. I didn't think I recognized the name, but I wanted to be sure."

Suddenly, a thought occurred to Joelle. "What if he didn't admit her with her real name? Someone might discover her that way."

"That would only be possible if he had the appropriate documents," Emily said. "Is that something he could have managed?"

Carter nodded. "There's no limit to what this man could manage."

"Okay," Emily said, "then let's take a look by time. Give me a year and month to start."

Alaina gave her the year and month they were told their mother died. Emily tapped on the keyboard again, then scrolled through records. Joelle was about to give the whole thing up as a rabbit trail when Emily put her finger on the screen.

"Only one woman around your mother's age was

admitted at that time. Name is Mary Parker. That mean anything to any of you?"

Joelle looked over at Alaina and Danae, who both shook their head. "No," Joelle said, "but he would have used a name that couldn't be traced to her family or to himself, right? Why was she admitted?"

Emily blew out a breath. "Without knowing for sure she's your mother, I can't give out any information about her condition."

"But surely," Joelle said, "that doesn't matter after death."

Emily's eyes widened and she looked at each of them. "Mary Parker isn't dead."

Joelle sucked in a breath as Danae grabbed her hand and squeezed. "You're certain?" Joelle asked.

"Positive," Emily said. "She's still a resident here. The staff always thought it odd that she never had a single family member visit her, but this might explain it all. I can arrange for you to see her...if you're prepared for that."

"Yes." All three of them spoke at once and Emily rose from her desk. "Now, I don't want you to get your hopes up. This woman may be someone completely different."

"We understand," Alaina said, "and we're ready to accept whatever comes of this, but we need to know for sure, either way."

Emily gave them a single nod and picked up the

phone. She gave a brief explanation of the situation, then went silent. Joelle held her breath, hoping they weren't refused access. Finally, Emily hung up the phone and rose from her desk.

"I can take you up myself," she said and waved them out of the office.

They all followed Emily down the hall and crowded on the elevator. "Mary stopped speaking shortly after she got here. Shocked the heck out of everyone when she started trying to again a couple of months ago. I've said a few words to her myself. She has always been such a sweet lady, but so sad it hurts even looking at her. I have to admit, I hope you're her family. Maybe she can get better."

"You have no idea what's wrong with her?" Joelle asked.

Emily shrugged. "One of the nurse's aides said she thought she was paranoid schizophrenic, but maybe what everyone thought was paranoia was the truth, huh? Wouldn't that be something?"

She stopped at a large steel door and tapped a code into a security panel. Joelle heard a loud click and Emily pushed the door open and waved them inside, then ensured the door closed and locked behind them. Joelle crossed her arms across her chest, a chill running through her at the thought of being locked in this sterile environment for twenty-five years.

"Since there's so many of you, her nurse thought

it would be better to bring her into the activity room. It's empty right now, so you'll have plenty of privacy." She stopped in front of a door. "Are you ready?"

They all nodded, and Emily pushed the door open so that they could walk inside.

A nurse stood beside a chair, positioned near a plate-glass window overlooking a courtyard. The woman in the chair peered out the window, her long black-and-silver hair tied back in a ponytail.

Then she turned.

Alaina clutched Joelle's arm as Joelle gasped.

"I don't believe it," Danae whispered.

The woman focused on them and her eyes widened. She pushed herself up from the chair and walked toward them, the shock on her face turning to excitement with every step. They stood stock-still, none of them able to move.

Mother!

Life had taken her youth, but it couldn't take her delicate bone structure. Joelle would have recognized her face anywhere and at any age. As she stepped in front of them, her eyes shone and tears collected in her eyes.

"My girls," she whispered.

Those two words broke the spell and all three of them reached for her as they collapsed into tears. But this time, it was tears of joy.

Epilogue

Christmas Eve

Joelle ran down the kitchen hallway, pulling her heels on as she went. "They're here," she called out and looked up at the balcony. Tyler started down the stairs and she sucked in a breath at how gorgeous he looked in his black tuxedo.

He grinned at her as he ran down the stairs and lifted her up to twirl her around. "Have I told you yet how stunning you are in this dress?"

The dress was navy blue sequined and designed to fit every curve of her body, and Joelle knew she looked good in it. "Not in the last ten minutes," she said with a smile.

"Have I told you how I can't wait to get you out of it?"

She laughed. "Party first. Private celebration later."

He put her down and gave her a lingering kiss. "Promise?"

"It's going to be the highlight of my night."

"Really?" He lifted her hand to see the sparkling diamond he'd placed on her finger earlier. "I thought this was the highlight."

She looked down at the ring and sighed, unable to help herself. "A girl's allowed more than one highlight on such a special occasion. Now, come on, before they start banging on the door." She grabbed his hand and pulled him to the front door.

She could already hear the voices outside as car doors slammed. Wave number one of the party guests had arrived. The first hour was for family—the people closest to the sisters and Ophelia—then after that, the entire town was invited to the celebration.

Joelle pulled open the door and beamed at everyone as they made their way toward the house. Carter and Alaina, looking every bit the golden couple they were. Zach and Danae, beautifully matched and so clearly in love. Amos, no longer on crutches but still refusing any help from his niece, who tried to assist him up the steps. Johnny, carrying a tray of food even though he'd been told only to bring himself.

The last couple made Joelle's heart swell with joy—William and Willamina.

Willamina was simply breathtaking in a long white sequined gown, and William was every bit his son's father in his black tuxedo. She had her hand on his arm and as they walked, he looked down at her, his adoration apparent in his smile.

"Look at my dad," Tyler whispered.

Joelle slipped her hand in Tyler's and gave it a squeeze. "I'm so glad you pushed him. They're made for each other."

Everyone filed up the steps, pausing only long enough to hug Joelle and exclaim over her ring before entering the house. Gasps filled the entry as they collected in the center of the large room, gazing around with obvious delight.

The house was returned to its previous splendor. A thirty-foot tree sat at the back of the entry, its top almost reaching the vaulted ceiling. It glittered with white and silver ribbons and decorations. Thick garland made from real pine trees wove around the balconies and down the spiral staircase. Silver ribbon and white poinsettias that matched the tree adorned it.

When everything unfolded to the Calais residents, the entire town was stunned by the extent of Purcell's crimes and the number of Calais locals who had participated. They were equally surprised and thrilled that Ophelia was alive and back home where she belonged, but saddened that she'd lost so many years of her life locked away in a facility where she finally chose silence because no one would listen.

"It's beautiful," Alaina said. "Is everything ready?"

"Yes, it's been amazing how everyone in Calais pitched in and helped get the house ready. I can't believe all of this was accomplished in less than two months."

"Now that all the bad guys and ghosts are gone, people are happy to be here," Alaina said.

Danae looked around the beautiful room and smiled. "Next year, your first occupants will be moving in. I can't believe this former monstrosity is going to be a beautiful safe haven for abused women. It's such a wonderful thing you're doing, Joelle."

Joelle sniffed. "I couldn't have done it without you. After all, the house belonged to Mother and you've both invested some of your own trust funds in this."

"And I've never been happier to write a check in my life," Alaina said as Danae nodded in agreement.

Joelle reached out to grab her sisters' hands. "Let's go get Mother. She's been primping forever. It's time for her to get out here and see the people who care about her."

They headed to a newly remodeled bedroom at

the back of the entry and Joelle knocked lightly on the door before poking her head inside. "Mom, it's us," she said and the three sisters slipped inside.

Ophelia stepped out of the bathroom and they all stared. She wore a long dress of satin and sequined teal. Joelle had called her genius hairstylist for an on-site consultation, and she'd trimmed Ophelia's long locks and eliminated the silver, restoring her hair to the lustrous black they remembered.

Her skin had developed a healthy glow from working outside, planting flowers alongside her daughters, but she'd kept hidden while the contractors and Calais locals were in the house, not yet steady enough to face everyone.

Ophelia didn't have an answer for how she'd been able to appear to each of them—only that she concentrated all of her will on making it happen and was sometimes able to see them, even speak. She'd also seen the other spirit—the one they thought was Purcell—and had driven him away. Since she'd returned to her home, no one had seen the bad spirit, and they all hoped that meant they were rid of Trenton Purcell once and for all.

"Mother, you're breathtaking," Alaina said.

Ophelia looked in the dresser mirror and pulled at a tendril of hair. "I don't know. This dress is cut so low and I'm not sure about my hair."

"Your hair is gorgeous," Danae said.

Joelle nodded. "And we have just the thing to take attention away from that low-cut dress."

Alaina pulled a velvet jewelry box from her purse and handed it to their mother. She gave them a questioning look.

"Just open it," Alaina said.

She lifted the lid, then her hand went up to cover her mouth. "How did you find it? He told me he sold it." She lifted the necklace out of the box—the necklace that matched the one in the painting.

"We didn't find the original," Alaina said. "But Joelle remembered where the uncut diamonds were."

Ophelia's eyes widened. "The purple bag. I can't believe I'd forgotten."

"Those stones brought you a lot of pain," Joelle said. "It's no wonder that you would compartmentalize them and lock that memory away."

"But with the stones discovered and the painting to guide us on design," Danae continued, "we were able to have a new necklace made—to replace the one that was taken from you."

"Let me fasten it," Alaina said, and stepped around behind their mother to fasten the necklace. She hooked the necklace in place, then stepped back around to stand beside her sisters.

The necklace glimmered at Ophelia's neck, but it came nowhere near to matching the brilliance of her smile.

* * * * *

LARGER-PRINT BOOKS!
GET 2 FREE LARGER-PRINT NOVELS PLUS
2 FREE GIFTS!

HARLEQUIN

INTRIGUE

BREATHTAKING ROMANTIC SUSPENSE

HILPI3R